Praise for *The Crown of Solomon:*

WHILE READING Rabbi Marc Angel's *The Crown of Solomon and Other Stories,* I could not stop wondering whether David Barukh, the unrecognized Sephardic Mozart, was a metaphor for the last two centuries of the Ottoman Sephardic culture, a metaphor for all the wasted opportunities and unrealized potentials! Rabbi Angel's stories demonstrate that Sepharadim can still teach modern American readers a thing or two, a lesson in honesty, or modesty—or, maybe, how to turn a defect into effect. Rabbi Angel does not idealize his Sephardic characters, not even the rabbinic ones. Some of his rabbis, like Hakham Shelomo, are wise in an a *la turca* way; others are quite average, like Hakham Ezra; some are humble, honorable and even saintly like Rabbi Bejerano—and yet others are frivolous and self-centered, like Rabbi Tedeschi. All are convincingly human and quite imaginable in real life. The lay characters of the stories are simply conquering in their charming simplicity, in their human rootedness and in their folk wisdom. While reading Rabbi Marc Angel's new book, I felt everything was in its place. It takes a person deeply rooted in both cultures, traditional Sephardic and modern American, to tell so Sephardic a story in a language such as English, and who makes everything feel totally right.

— Dr. Eliezer Papo, Head of the Sephardic Studies Research Institute, Ben-Gurion University of the Negev

The Crown of Solomon
and Other Stories

Marc D. Angel

Albion
Andalus
Boulder, Colorado
2014

"The old shall be renewed,
and the new shall be made holy."
— Rabbi Avraham Yitzhak Kook

"Sacred Music" was originally published in issue 11 (Autumn 2011) of *Conversations,* the journal of the Institute for Jewish Ideas and Ideals, under the pen name Marco de Falquera.

Albion-Andalus, Inc.
P. O. Box 19852
Boulder, CO 80308
www.albionandalus.com

Design and layout by Albion-Andalus Books
Cover design by Sari Wisenthal-Shore

ISBN-13: 978-0615997254 (Albion-Andalus Books)
ISBN-10: 0615997252

DEDICATION

To my family and friends,
to teachers and students,
. . . to all whose love and loyalty
have sustained me,
. . . to all my readers.

Contents

ACKNOWLEDGEMENTS

I THANK NETANEL MILES-YÉPEZ of Albion-Andalus Books for inviting me to write this collection of stories. His thoughtfulness and encouragement have made this book possible. I would also like to thank Dr. Jane Mushabac for her helpful editorial comments.

I am indebted to my teachers and to the many authors whose works I have read over the years, each of whom has influenced me and my work in some way. I make special mention of my first literature professor at Yeshiva College, Dr. Maurice Wohlgelernter. The "Reb," as he was known by students, was a masterful and exuberant teacher. Our friendship continued for nearly fifty years until his passing in June 2013. His memory is a source of strength and blessing.

I was born and raised in the Sephardic community of Seattle, Washington. While both of my parents—Victor B. and Rachel Romey Angel—were born in Seattle, my paternal grandparents—Bohor Yehuda and Bulissa Esther Huniu Angel—had come from the Island of Rhodes early in the 20th-century. My maternal grandparents arrived from Turkey during that same time-period. My grandfather Marco Romey had come from Tekirdag and my grandmother Sultana Policar had emigrated from the Island of Marmara. Growing up in the extended Angel-Romey family clan, among many Sephardim of Judeo-Spanish background, is a privilege for which I am profoundly grateful. Many of the stories in this book reflect the Judeo-Spanish civilization in which I was nurtured.

My wife, Gilda, has been the love, light and blessing of my life; I owe her far more than words can express. I thank our children Rabbi Hayyim and Maxine Siegel Angel, Dr. Dan and Ronda Angel Arking, and Dr. James and Elana Angel Nussbaum for their ongoing love and devotion. I thank our grandchildren, each of whom is so unique and precious: Jake Nussbaum, Andrew Arking, Jonathan Marc Arking, Max Nussbaum, Charles Nussbaum, Jeremy Arking, Kara Nussbaum, Aviva Hayya Angel, and Dahlia Rachel Angel.

I thank the Almighty for all His blessings and for having brought me to this special time.

— M. D. A.

INTRODUCTION

SHORT STORIES POSE IDEAS, emotions, or enigmas that strive to engage readers in an exploration of the complexities of human life. While each author has a distinctive approach to this literary genre, my own view is that stories should be spare, clear and poignant. They should avoid flowery language and superfluous descriptions. Upon reading a story, the reader should experience an insight, a jolt, even a feeling of slight puzzlement. And then a feeling of clarity.

The stories in this volume are drawn from the old world and the new world. While set in particular places and times, they relate to many times and places; they relate to the realities in which we live here and now.

Most of the stories are fictional. They involve characters and events fashioned by the author's imagination. Although fictional, they are "true" in the sense of being authentic representations of the worlds that they describe. There was no real Hakham Shelomo Yahalomi in Izmir; yet the fictional Hakham Shelomo is as true to Izmir life as though he had actually lived there. Likewise for David Barukh, Sultana Abulafia, Rabbi Tsadik

Bejerano, Luz Alvarez and the other characters in this book. They are fictional, but true.

The story "Murder" is not fiction. This is my retelling of a story within our family's history recalling the life and death of my Uncle Joseph and family. Although they died before I was born, their story and their lives continue to matter.

"Leader of the Jewish People," "The Wedding," and "Uncle Moshe's House" are my recounting of actual events from my own memory. Stories of the imagination and stories of history do ultimately share literary territory; they are reflections of the human adventure.

— MARC D. ANGEL, NEW YORK

The Crown of Solomon
and Other Stories

THE CROWN OF SOLOMON

HAKHAM SHELOMO YAHALOMI was the jewel in the crown of the Jews of Izmir during the early 19th century. A luminous scholar, a sainted kabbalist, a genius: Hakham Shelomo was venerated and loved by his community.

He was neither too tall nor too short; neither too heavy nor too thin. Everything about him was balanced and harmonious. He dressed in the traditional style of Chief Rabbis of the Ottoman Empire with turban and embroidered gown, but he also sometimes wore European style suits and hats. He seemed always to be busy with his studies, and yet always to have time for everyone, young and old. Hakham Shelomo Yahalomi was a unique treasure.

He had many disciples, but none so devoted as Matatya Kerido. Matatya was the acknowledged "second in command". Matatya had studied for many years as the prize student of Hakham Shelomo; the two loved and understood each other. They were like father and son. Indeed, Matatya was the substitute for the son Hakham Shelomo and his wife were not blessed to have. The Yahalomis were childless.

Although he dedicated long hours to his studies and his communal responsibilities, Hakham

Shelomo devoted several hours each day to work on his magnum opus. During those hours, no one was allowed to disturb him, no matter how great the emergency. During those hours—so the people said—Hakham Shelomo discussed the deep mysteries of the Torah with the angels. He was working on his life's work, a book plumbing the profoundest secrets of Torah, *halakha* and *kabbala*. It was said that he offered his insights to the visiting angels, gaining their approval before he wrote down even one word. Such was the holiness of Hakham Shelomo Yahalomi, spiritual leader of the holy congregation of Izmir.

Hakham Shelomo named his opus *Keter Shelomo*, "Solomon's Crown." From time to time he would mention his book; but never did he show a single page of it to anyone, not even to his beloved disciple Matatya Kerido. When Matatya hinted at his desire to see the manuscript, his teacher said: "You will see *Keter Shelomo* in good time, after it is completed." When Matatya offered to raise funds to arrange publication of *Keter Shelomo*, Hakham Shelomo said: "We will not speak of publication until the work is completed. It is still far from complete."

As the years passed, some of the rabbis and Torah students began to murmur against Hakham Shelomo. At first, these murmurings were whispered privately among the scholars. Soon, though, they became fodder for public gossip. Voices were raised: if Hakham Shelomo has attained such great wisdom, why does he not share it with us? If his manuscript

Keter Shelomo is being written with the help of angels, why does he deprive us of its lessons? He is selfish; he does not really care about us; he would rather speak with angels than with us! He refuses to publish his work because he thinks we are unworthy or unable to understand it.

Matatya sought to quell the growing chorus of criticisms. He reminded his fellow rabbis, scholars and members of the holy community of Izmir: Hakham Shelomo has taught Torah to us for many years. We all have learned much from him. We know from his lectures and sermons how brilliant he is, how much Torah he knows, how deep is his wisdom. He is selfless and sharing; he has time for each of us; he loves each of us. More than we want to learn from him, he wants to teach us. It is ridiculous to accuse him of being selfish. If he does not publish *Keter Shelomo*, he must have good reasons. Perhaps the angels have forbidden him to publish the book for now. Perhaps he wants it to be perfect before issuing it to the public. We must not cast aspersions on the holiness and piety of our great Hakham Shelomo Yahalomi, jewel in the crown of our holy congregation of Izmir. Woe unto those who cast suspicion on the reputation of the righteous! Woe unto those who question the powers of our great Hakham Shelomo Yahalomi.

Yet, in the back of his mind, Matatya was not at ease in defending his rabbi and teacher. He, too, felt that Hakham Shelomo should publish the book for the benefit of the public. And, although he would not admit this even to himself, Matatya felt hurt that Hakham Shelomo would not let him see the manuscript. He was Hakham Shelomo's most devoted, most beloved disciple, almost like a son— and yet Hakham Shelomo kept Matatya outside the inner sanctum of his spiritual life.

One day, Hakham Shelomo said to Matatya: "I know that there is gossip in the community about *Keter Shelomo*. Tell them that soon they will see my manuscript. I have worked many years on *Keter Shelomo*. During the first years of my work, I was expansive; I tried to explain and interpret as comprehensively and clearly as I could. In the ensuing years, I have worked to refine and purify and distill; I have sought the essence of wisdom and holiness and truth in their most lucid form. To you, Matatya—my disciple and my 'son'—I will leave the *Keter Shelomo* as an inheritance. You will be the first to see it; and you will convey it to the public."

Several weeks after this conversation, Hakham Shelomo took ill. Although he knew that death was imminent, he remained serene; his eyes retained their sparkle; his mind was clear and focused. He spent precious hours with his beloved manuscript. When he was satisfied that he had at last completed the *Keter Shelomo,* he put it into a box, tied the box shut, and placed a note on it: "For my disciple and son, Matatya Kerido." With his manuscript completed, Hakham Shelomo died in peace.

All the members of the community—men and women, young and old, admirers and critics—

attended the funeral of Hakham Shelomo Yahalomi. The saintly, wise and loving sage of Izmir was laid to rest in the old Jewish cemetery, in the row reserved for the community's rabbis. As per his instructions, his tombstone was to include only his name, dates of birth and death, and the words: "Author of the *Keter Shelomo.*"

During the seven-day mourning period, prayers were chanted in the Hakham's home each morning and evening. His widow was surrounded by neighbors and friends who came to console her. Matatya spent these days in the house of mourning, as though he were a son grieving the death of his father.

On the night concluding the seven day mourning period, known among Izmir's Jews as *corte de siete*, prayers were chanted in the home for the last time. After the memorial prayer was recited, refreshments were served to the many guests—sweet rolls, Greek olives, raisins, hard boiled eggs, sliced tomatoes. People ate, chatted, reminisced—and gradually left the home.

By the end of the evening, the widow was alone with Matatya and five of the city's rabbis and scholars who had lingered on in the hope of seeing the *Keter Shelomo*. During the days of mourning, no one had dared to ask to see the manuscript.

"Come Matatya. Come rabbis," said the widow in a hushed voice. "Now it is time for you to have the *Keter Shelomo*. It is in a box on Hakham Shelomo's desk in his study upstairs. He told me that it is bequeathed to Matatya, and that Matatya would understand its significance."

Matatya and the rabbis climbed the wooden steps and entered the book-lined room of Hakham Shelomo. The room was in perfect order. The only item on the desk was the box containing the *Keter Shelomo*.

Matatya slowly approached the manuscript, his heart racing. The others followed close behind him in eager anticipation. He lifted the box, untied the string that held it shut, and opened it. Inside he found just one page, a blank page, a tear-stained page without a single word written on it.

He quickly glanced around the desk to see if there were other pages, if there was another box. No, this was the *Keter Shelomo*. There were no other pages, no other box. This single page was the entire product of Hakham Shelomo Yahalomi's years of study; this was his wisdom and his legacy.

One of the rabbis, a vindictive gleam in his eye, called out: "You see: the *Keter Shelomo* is nothing. Hakham Shelomo Yahalomi left us nothing."

Matatya held the white, tear-stained page lovingly and with a sense of profound wonder. "No," said Matatya, "Hakham Shelomo has left us everything. The *Keter Shelomo* is everything."

SACRED MUSIC

DAVID BARUKH was born January 27, 1756, the same day as Wolfgang Amadeus Mozart. Yet, David Barukh never heard of Mozart, never even heard a note of Mozart's music.

David Barukh was born to poor parents in the tiny Jewish community of the Island of Rhodes. The "Rhodeslies" (as the Jews of Rhodes were known in the Judeo-Spanish civilization of the Ottoman Empire) were a proud group of 300 or so families, many tracing themselves back to ancestors from the golden age of medieval Spanish Jewry. The Rhodeslies had a respectable number of rabbinic scholars and prosperous merchants; and an excessively large number of indigent Jews who eked out livelihoods as peddlers, shop keepers, and hamalim (stevedores) on the docks of Rhodes. David's father was a ne'er do well who supported his wife and six children primarily by receiving stipends from the communal charity fund.

It is not likely that any of the Jews of the Island of Rhodes had heard of Mozart or would have appreciated his music. They lived in their own world, with their own Judeo-Spanish language, their own traditions and way of life. They were enclosed by the walls of the old city of Rhodes; Rhodes was an island not only physically, but also culturally.

David was the youngest of the six Barukh children—twenty years younger than his oldest brother Mushon and twelve years younger than his next older sibling, his sister Sarina. By all accounts, he was a surprise to his parents; the more malicious gossips said he was a mistake. He was given the name David, after a long deceased uncle who had lived an unfortunate life and who died childless.

For most of his childhood, David Barukh felt quite alone. His father stayed out of the house long hours, pretending to be at work. His mother, a morose woman, who looked far older than her thirty-eight years, had little patience for her youngest child. She thought she was done with the rigors of childbirth and child-rearing, and now she was stuck with a new mouth to feed, a new source of noise in the already raucous household. She never overcame her feelings of antipathy toward her youngest child. David's siblings were much older than he, and spent little time with him.

Perhaps if David had been a cute, loveable child, things would have been different. But he was not blessed with charm. He was homely, even as a baby. He had a screeching high-pitched voice. He was moody. As he grew up, these negative features became harsher and more annoying. When he was sent to the *meldar*, the elementary school for Jewish boys, he antagonized teachers and fellow students alike. He sank deeper and deeper into isolation. The only time he seemed to be happy was when he was left alone.

By age thirteen, David had dropped out of school. Although he had learned to read the prayers in Hebrew, and had gained a smattering of knowledge relating to the Bible and rabbinic lore, he could barely write or make the simplest mathematical calculations. His parents had little hope for his future; his teachers had given up on him; everyone assumed he would end up as an unskilled, indigent worker—or as a beggar.

But David knew deep in his soul that the Lord was his Rock, that God had not forgotten or abandoned him. He felt the warmth of God's love, especially when he wandered alone along the sandy shoreline of the Aegean Sea, just outside the walls of the Old City and its Jewish Quarter. God had given David a profound, mysterious power.

This power was music.

From a very early age, David could hear music in his mind; he could hear incredible harmonies. He would start humming a melody, become entranced by it, create variations on it; he could imagine a chorus of a thousand voices singing the melody; he could hear the high voices and the low voices; he could feel the overwhelming power, the overwhelming joy, the sheer transcendence of the music. When David heard this inner music, he knew he was in God's presence, that God had not forgotten him. He may have been an insignificant pauper in an isolated island—but God had not forgotten him.

As he grew older, David spent more and more time with his inner music. He became increasingly alienated from those few people who still cared about him. He slept in a small corner of his parent's home; he ate meager rations of food; he dressed in old, tattered clothing. But these things did not bother him. As long as he had his music, he was happy. God was his Rock and Redeemer. He did not need anything else.

When he turned eighteen, his parents decided it was time for David to be married. But who would give their daughter in marriage to David, this strange young man with such poor prospects for supporting a wife and family? They sent David to their rabbi, Hakham Ezra, for guidance.

Hakham Ezra was an elderly and stern sage who had been spiritual leader of the Jews of Rhodes for many years. Hakham Ezra knew David from infancy; he knew the family; he knew the difficulties. When David came to see him, Hakham Ezra came right to the point.

"David, you are now eighteen years old. It is time for you to think of marrying. We need to find you a suitable wife; but you first need to prepare yourself for the new responsibilities. You need to find work; you need to be focused. You live in a dream-world, David; but it's time for you to grow up."

David was not listening to Hakham Ezra. Instead, he was entranced by a mysterious new melody that had engulfed his mind. It was so exquisite: soft, lilting, filled with love, filled with sweetness. David closed his eyes so as to better concentrate on this inner music.

Hakham Ezra saw that David had not heard a word that had been said to him. He coughed to get David's attention; but David was lost in his own inner world of music. At last, Hakham Ezra spoke again to David: "David, listen to me. I am speaking with you and I expect you to pay attention."

An indescribable sadness filled David's face. Hakham Ezra's voice had driven out the music. The spell had been broken, and David felt robbed and betrayed. Hakham Ezra saw that something had snapped within David. "What's the matter with you, David? Why do you suddenly look so sad? Are you upset that I brought up the issue of your getting married?"

"No, Hakham Ezra. I did not even hear you speaking of marriage. You don't understand me. No one understands me."

"Explain yourself. Help me to understand you. I am your rabbi. I want to help you."

"I have a special power within me. I hear music, beautiful, unimaginably beautiful music. I wish I could share it with you, with others—but I cannot. The music is locked in my head and it has no way out. I can hum the melodies, but my humming is only a faint reflection of what I actually hear in my mind."

"Don't talk nonsense, David. This is exactly your problem: you imagine music in your head, and therefore, you don't concentrate on what is really important. Push this music out of your mind; it is the evil inclination trying to deflect you from your responsibilities. You need a job. You need to marry and start a family of your own. You need to outgrow your childhood fantasies."

David heard the words of Hakham Ezra and felt as though daggers were piercing through his heart. "My music is not nonsense," he said quietly but forcefully. "It is a gift that God has given to me. Please, Hakham Ezra, please help me. You are a sage, a great scholar. You know many things. Tell me how I can bring this music out of my mind, how I can share it with others, how this music can bring greater glory to God."

"Take my advice, David, and drive this music from your mind. Try to find work. Let us seek to find you a good wife. Perhaps you can hope to live a normal life, and not be condemned to be a vagabond."

"I cannot drive the music from my mind, and I don't wish to drive it away. It brings me great happiness. I want to share this music. I want to release it from my mind and let others enjoy it. I want to sing a new song in praise of God."

Hakham Ezra tossed up his hands in despair. "If you keep speaking of your music, David, there isn't much I can do to help you. You are going on a bad path. You will end up a broken man. You need to come to your senses."

David arose, nodded his head gently, and left the presence of Hakham Ezra. A thick, nagging sadness filled his soul. But then a melody flashed into his mind, and he started to hum. Happiness and calmness returned. The Lord was his Rock and Redeemer. The Lord prepared him for the battles of life by giving him music.

Realizing that Hakham Ezra did not make headway with David, his parents sent him to see Hazzan Eliezer, the leader of prayers at the Kahal Shalom synagogue. Hazzan Eliezer was a heavy-set, plodding middle-aged man of mediocre intellect. He was blessed, though, with a pleasant voice, so that he was appointed as the *hazzan* (cantor) of the synagogue. He chanted the prayers clearly; he read the Torah with remarkable accuracy. David's parents hoped that perhaps Hazzan Eliezer would talk some sense into David, and maybe even consider training him to be an assistant reader of services. This would enable David to earn a salary, however small, and put him on the right path for a responsible life.

"Please help me, Hazzan Eliezer," David began. "I hear wonderful music in my mind, so powerful that it overwhelms me. I do not know how to get others to hear this music. I can hum a tune, but is only a frail echo of what I hear. I hear hundreds, thousands of voices. I hear tremendous harmonies. I want this music to bring glory to God."

Hazzan Eliezer was skeptical. "Well, David, please hum one of the melodies for me. Maybe I'll have a better idea of how to help you if I first hear your music."

David's eyes lit up. "I'll hum a tune that is just right for the *Nishmath* (the opening prayer of the Sabbath morning service)." As he hummed in his high-pitched squeaky voice, David's eyes closed, he stood on his tiptoes, he lifted his arms and waved them as though he were conducting a vast choir. He hummed until tears came to his eyes, tears of ineffable joy. When he completed his rendition of *Nishmath*, he slowly came back to consciousness. As he opened his eyes, he saw Hazzan Eliezer's disapproving face.

"First," said Hazzan Eliezer, "the tune is no good. It wanders here and there, and is painful to follow. No one will be able to sing it. We are not accustomed to such music. Second, we don't need new tunes for the *Nishmath*—or for any other part of our prayers. We have traditional melodies that everyone loves; everyone is happy and comfortable with them. No one wants new tunes, especially tunes like yours which have neither beginning nor end. We have our musical traditions, our *makams*, and these are the essence of beautiful music. What you have hummed is outlandish. It doesn't fit. It is no good."

"You don't understand, Hazzan Eliezer," David said with tears in his eyes. "You don't understand, and no one understands."

David was determined to find someone who would understand, who would listen to his music, who would help him find a way to release his inner music for the benefit of others and for the glory of God. He stopped people in the market place and hummed his melodies; people walked away from him, pitying him as a hopeless fool. He stood in the center of the broad square in the middle of the Jewish Quarter, the *calle ancha*, and sang loudly. The passersby rushed right past him. They did not hear him, or did not want to hear him.

His parents gave up on him. His siblings had no use for him. The members of the community thought he was a lunatic. He had no future. He was a lost soul. He was destined to be a beggar, an outcast.

But David stayed faithful to his inner music. In his mind, he composed music, sacred music set to biblical and liturgical texts. He sang a new melody, which became his favorite, to the words of the Psalmist: "Lord, what is man that You take knowledge of him, the child of mortals that You take thought of him? Man is like a breath, his days are as a passing shadow." He sang this new song again and again as he walked the narrow streets of the Jewish Quarter, as he stood by the statue of seahorses in the *calle ancha*, as he begged for alms, as he cried himself to sleep at night in a corner of his parent's home. The new melody was haunting, powerful beyond words; if only others would listen to it, if only they would take the music into their souls. But no one listened, and no one cared, and no one's soul was touched by the beauty of David's music.

Years passed. David's parents died. His siblings maintained the parents' home, so that David would have a place to sleep, a place to call home. They were ashamed of him—but he was their brother and they felt obliged to help him as best they could. He tried to make his siblings understand him, hear his music—but they were not interested. David was an unfortunate case, a madman. He was their burden.

David continued to hear and to create music in his mind. He wanted the music—a gift of God— to be devoted to the glory of God. He composed a massive repertoire of religious music. Although he could only sing the compositions in his feeble, high pitched voice, in his mind he heard it being sung by a vast choir—a choir of many voices, a choir of angelic beauty and solemnity. Within himself, he was blessed and happy. The Lord was his Rock and Redeemer. Yet, he was infinitely sad that his greatest treasure—his God-given music—was trapped within himself alone, and that not a single soul listened to it or understood it or was moved by it.

One day, for no apparent reason, the music stopped within David's mind. He listened intently, he strained with all his concentration—but there was only silence. His entire life had been infused by this divine music; the music had been his sustenance, his only joy and fulfillment. He sang many of the songs that he had composed in the past, to see if his singing would re-ignite his inner music. But nothing happened. He sang his old songs, over and over; but they were frail and uninspired. When he had sung these songs previously, he could hear a glorious choir in his mind singing along with him. Now, his voice was a thin reed, without choral accompaniment.

"Lord," David cried, "send forth Your hands from

on high; rescue me, deliver me from the great flood." But there was no response; there was no rescue. The music was gone.

Without his music, David's life became empty, frightening, ugly. His homely countenance was constantly downcast. He no longer stopped passersby to sing for them; he no longer stood in the *calle ancha* chanting his compositions in praise of the Almighty. He ambled aimlessly through the streets; he sought solace walking along the sea shore. His eyes filled with tears; his Rock and Redeemer had taken away the music. David had failed. He had received the most precious of gifts, but he had not known how to communicate it. No one had listened, no one had cared, no one could help him bring his music into the hearts and souls of others.

Without his inner music, life was not worth living. Alone and abandoned, David prayed for his death. He repeatedly hummed his favorite song: "Lord, what is man that You take knowledge of him, the child of mortals that You take thought of him? Man is like a breath, his days are as a passing shadow."

David Barukh, gifted musical genius, was a broken and ruined man.

One winter day, he walked through the gate of the walls surrounding the Old City of Rhodes, outside the Jewish Quarter. He strolled along the sandy seashore, and stared out at the rhythmic ocean waves. A deep serenity set in. And then, miraculously, his head filled with music, the most powerful music he had ever experienced. He heard thousands and thousands of voices, incredible harmonies; his soul leaped with joy; his heart filled with rapture. The Lord was his Rock and Redeemer; the Lord had not forgotten him. Not only had the Lord given him back his inner music, but He had given it back on a level beyond compare, more beautiful, more enigmatic, more entrancing than anything David had ever heard or imagined before.

David Barukh had never felt happier or more blessed in his entire life. This was the crescendo, the climax of his inner music. He stared into the sea, intoxicated by the ethereal music, music that was beyond what a human soul could bear; it was the music of angels. David Barukh felt his heart and soul surge. He fell to the sand, dead.

David Barukh died on December 5, 1791, the same day that Mozart died.

BETRAYAL AND REDEMPTION

SULTANA ABULAFIA was a beautiful but frail thirteen-year-old girl. She lived with her parents, three older sisters and one older brother in a simple stucco house on the Island of Marmara, Turkey. She and her family were among the several hundred Jewish souls living on the Island, all of whom were Judeo-Spanish speakers whose ancestors had been expelled from Spain in 1492. This small Jewish community lived among a much larger community of Greek Orthodox Christians, as well as about a thousand Turkish Muslims.

Most of the residents of Marmara were involved in fishing, small scale agriculture, artisan trades, peddling, and storekeeping. There were very few rich residents in town and a great many poor. Each community—Greek, Turkish and Jewish—tended to live in its own section of town, having little social interaction with members of the other groups. In the world of business, though, members of the three groups interacted frequently and easily.

Marmara was a scenic and sunny locale, blessed with a marvelous coastline of sandy beaches. An abundance of trees and flowers filled the town and countryside. The hills that surrounded the town were green and inviting. Life in Marmara was generally calm and uneventful.

When Sultana was born in 1895, she weighed barely five pounds. While her siblings all grew up strong and healthy, Sultana was small and sickly throughout her childhood. She was sweet and kind . . . but she was self-conscious of her physical weakness. She preferred to be alone so as not to let others observe her condition. Her poor health impacted negatively on her emotional and social life; she thought little of herself; she was overly shy and reticent.

In those days, girls did not attend schools. They learned what they needed to know from their mothers at home. So Sultana had a very quiet and sheltered life, with little interaction with anyone outside her family.

There was one exception.

Not far from the Abulafia's home lived a Greek family, the Stavolakis. The two families maintained formal neighborly relations, but Sultana developed a warm relationship with Maria Stavolakis. Sultana and Maria were about the same age. As they grew up, they spent much time with each other . . . chatting, playing, dreaming. Although they were from different religious backgrounds, they seemed to have kindred spirits.

Maria was the one real friend that Sultana had outside her immediate family. Maria was lively, healthy, athletic—qualities which Sultana lacked.

Maria had an endless storehouse of news, gossip and stories; Sultana drank in Maria's words with thirst and excitement. Although Sultana was shy by nature, Maria's spontaneous and natural manner gave Sultana the confidence to speak more often and more freely. The friendship went smoothly, except for one week each year when the girls did not see one another.

During Easter week, the Greek Orthodox community—led by its religious leaders—became inflamed with anti-Jewish passion. Jews went into hiding and stayed out of the way of Greek mobs during that week. Jews boarded the windows of their houses to protect against rocks hurled by Greek teenagers. They closed their shops and locked them tight. They stored enough food in their homes to carry them through the week so that they would not have to walk through the streets and face the inevitable abuse of Greek ruffians.

Once Easter week had passed, things would invariably return to "normal." Everything quieted down. Greeks and Jews resumed their usual business together as though nothing terrible had happened. The outrages of Easter week were simply taken for granted as a fact of life that one had to accept.

But things really never were totally comfortable between the two groups. On the surface, things looked fine; but below the surface, the Greeks harbored a deep, religion-based anti-Semitism, and the Jews therefore harbored a deep mistrust of the Greeks.

Although Sultana's parents wanted her to have friends, they were not happy that her best friend was Maria. They reminded Sultana that Jews could not trust Greeks, even those who seemed to be friendly. Maria could no more escape the poison of anti-Semitism than a tiger could give up its stripes. It was fine to spend time with Maria, as long as Sultana understood reality and maintained caution in her friendship. Sultana's parents sought to foster Sultana's friendships with Jewish children her age as a means of diminishing her dependence on Maria.

Nevertheless, Sultana and Maria remained close friends. As they entered their teen years, their friendship only seemed to deepen.

In the spring of 1908, the Jews of Marmara prepared for the festival of Passover, the celebration of the redemption of the ancient Israelites from their slavery in Egypt. For Sephardic Jews, the joy of remembering ancient miracles was marred by the nearer historic memory of the Edict of Expulsion of Jews from Spain, issued in March 1492 by King Ferdinand and Queen Isabella. Jews had lived in the Iberian Peninsula for a thousand years and had been a productive and creative element contributing to the greatness of medieval Spain. But the ugly anti-Semitism of the Spanish church made life miserable for Jews. In the name of religion, Jews were persecuted, robbed, murdered, or forcibly converted to Catholicism. The fires of hatred were fanned by priests and preachers, and the ignorant masses were only too happy to participate in the pogroms and plundering of Jews. Even when Jews adopted Catholicism, they were still subject to hatred; the vicious Inquisition hunted them down, imprisoned them, tortured them into confessions, and burnt them at the stake.

As the Spanish-speaking Jews of Marmara approached Passover, the festival of freedom, they were keenly aware of the fact that they still were not free. The lives of their ancestors in Spain had been uprooted by the Edict of Expulsion of 1492. So many Jews of those days died terrible deaths; so many were forcibly converted from their faith; so many were sent into exile. Among the descendants of those unhappy exiles were the Jews of Marmara. And these descendants faced their own horrors each year at Easter time . . . which generally coincided with the Passover festival. How could these Jews celebrate freedom when they suffered ongoing persecution, when the deep-seated anti-Jewish prejudices continued to be passed down from generation to generation?

On the first night of Passover 1908, Wednesday night April 15, the Jews of Marmara, like Jews throughout the world, sat around their dinner tables reciting the *Haggadah,* recounting the miraculous redemption of the ancient Israelites, singing songs, and eating a festive meal. But lurking in the back of their minds was the ominous shadow of the forthcoming observance of Easter and Easter week among the Greek Orthodox. The Holy Week before their Easter would begin on the Sunday of Passover, with Easter the following Sunday, and then Easter week thereafter. This was a perilous time for Jews.

In most years past, anti-Jewish outbreaks started on Easter and continued during the following week. But this year, things seemed to be heating up earlier. As Jews were preparing for Passover, they could sense the simmering hostility among their Greek neighbors and customers. Even as the Jews celebrated their festival of freedom, they were tense; they feared for their lives and the lives of their families. Yes, they had been through these episodes every year; and yes, they had always survived with minimum damage to life and property. Yet, this year they felt a particularly malevolent spirit in the air. They took more precautions than usual.

The Jews were a small group, far outnumbered by the Greeks. They were not accustomed to fighting. They saw their situation as a Divine punishment for past sins; they accepted their sufferings with passivity and with faith in their ultimate redemption by the Messiah. When they were attacked, they turned the other cheek.

Their passivity and unwillingness to fight made the Jews an easy target for Greek trouble makers. The villains knew they could act with impunity and not suffer any consequences. The government of Marmara would not defend Jews from Greek attacks. The Turks would not endanger themselves to help the Jews. The Jews were like a flock of sheep surrounded by hungry wolves.

On the morning of the second day of Passover,

Friday morning, the Jewish men were at synagogue for the prayer service. The women were busy at home readying things for the late morning meal when the men would be returning home. Sultana and her sisters had helped their mother, and now the women had an hour or so to rest quietly before the meal was to be served.

Sultana peeked out the window and saw a group of Greek girls talking and laughing. Maria was among them. Sultana felt an urge to go outside and be with Maria. She opened the front door of the house, but her mother immediately called out to her to shut the door and to stay inside. Even though this was not yet the dangerous time, it was close enough.

Sultana reminded her mother that Maria was among the girls on the street; Maria was a friend and she would look out for Sultana. Reluctantly, Sultana's mother agreed to let Sultana go outside.

As Sultana hesitantly walked toward the group of girls, Maria gave her a broad smile and invited her to come closer. Sultana felt emboldened by the kind gesture of her friend, and walked more quickly to join the group.

As she neared them, one of the Greek girls called out: "Christ killer!"

Sultana was confused, pained. She looked to Maria, hoping her friend would intercede.

"Christ killer!" the other girls shouted. "You little Jewish Christ killer."

Sultana started to back away from the group. But

Maria signaled her to come and stand next to her. So Sultana sidled her way past the girls to stand by her friend Maria.

Maria smiled at Sultana; and then suddenly punched her in the face. "Christ killer!" Maria screamed at Sultana.

Sultana's nose was bleeding. Her ears were ringing. She spun around in horrible pain—not simply from the physical blow she had received but from Maria's perfidious treason. As Sultana held back tears, the other girls followed Maria's lead, punching her, taunting her. "Christ killer!" they screamed as they made Sultana bleed.

The girls laughed at Sultana; Maria laughed loudest.

Suddenly, something clicked within Sultana's mind. Frail as she was, outnumbered as she was, she determined to fight back. She lunged at Maria and slapped her face with all the strength she could muster. Maria staggered backward, but then struck back at Sultana. The two girls fought ferociously, as the others cheered for their friend. Although Maria was so much stronger and was hitting so hard, Sultana would not surrender. At last, though, her strength gave out and she fell helplessly to the ground.

Maria and each of her friends kicked Sultana as she lay in the dirt. The girls ran away victoriously as they chanted "Christ killer, Christ killer!"

Sultana was badly beaten; but she did not cry.

Lying in the dirt, she felt stronger at that moment than at any other time in her life. Gradually, she picked herself back up and made her way home. Her mother and sisters were horrified to see her bloody and dirty. They cleaned her up, soothed her, cried for her, and cursed the wicked group of girls who had perpetrated this violence against an innocent and weak girl.

At age thirteen, having been beaten up by a group of anti-Semites, and having been betrayed by her best friend, Sultana felt a surge of power within her soul. She had fought back, she had struck Maria, she did not shrivel like a dry and trembling leaf. She discovered in herself courage that she had not imagined was possible for her.

When the family sat around the festive Passover table for their late morning meal, sadness and hopelessness filled their hearts—but not the heart of Sultana. She no longer was sad, and she no longer felt that things were hopeless.

She spoke: "The rabbi has taught us that we must suffer in silence as others abuse us and falsely accuse us. The rabbi has taught us that it is the will of God that we accept humiliation and pain as atonement for our sins. Today I learned that the rabbi has taught us false things. Today I learned that we can stand up for ourselves, we can fight back. When Maria punched me and her friends joined her, I suddenly seemed to understand things better. I realized that God could not want us to suffer such agony, that God would want us to act courageously as His chosen people. This Easter week, the Jews of Marmara must unboard our windows, open our stores, walk in the streets bravely. If attacked, we should fight back. If taunted, we should shout back. I will tell this to all our community; I will go from door to door and make people listen."

Indeed, that Easter week many Jews heeded Sultana's call. They did not board their windows. They kept their stores open. They fought back and shouted back at their oppressors. Some Jews were badly beaten up. Some Jewish stores were vandalized. Some Jewish homes had their windows shattered by stone-throwing bigots. Yet, a transformation had taken place.

The Jews of Marmara had found new strength and new courage. Instead of viewing themselves as helpless victims, they realized that they could and should defend themselves and protect their own interests.

Before the arrival of Easter week in 1909, Sultana and her siblings—along with other young Jews of Marmara—had joined the movement of young Jews who were becoming pioneers in the ancient Jewish homeland, in the land of Israel. Other young Jews moved to America. The elder Jews who remained in Marmara were proud of their young ones. The Jews of Marmara never again faced Easter week with fear.

In 1948, three of Sultana's sons and one of her daughters fought in Israel's War of Independence. The three sons all won distinction for heroism. The one daughter died courageously in battle, as she fought to protect fellow soldiers who had come under heavy enemy fire. That daughter's name was Maria.

PROGRESS

DURING THE FIRST decades of the twentieth century, Rabbi Tsadik Bejerano was the humble, saintly spiritual guide of the small Jewish community in Terkirdag, Turkey. He was not the "official" rabbi of the community. He took no salary, he demanded no honors. During the morning hours, he ran a small dry goods store in which he sold linens and blankets. The rest of the day, he devoted to teaching Torah, to ministering to the poor, the sick, the troubled.

He was an "old time" rabbi, such as used to lead Sephardic communities in the Ottoman Empire. He served as a matter of mission, not for any personal gain. He always was ready to listen to people's problems, to lend a hand, to offer words of faith and encouragement. He spoke in the traditional folksy Judeo-Spanish language, a language that was the mother tongue of the community going back hundreds of years. He was a beloved and respected personality.

But Rabbi Tsadik Bejerano represented the old times and the old ways. The new generation was restless for change. The affluent and cultured members of the community began to speak in French rather than Judeo-Spanish. Even if their hearts were still longing for their mother-tongue, they wanted their children to grow up modern in the French style. So they too put on French airs to set the example for their young. And to keep up with their children!

The world was changing for the Jews of Tekirdag. Many—especially the young from poor families—were leaving home to start new lives in America. The more "progressive" Jews were increasingly Francophile.

Rabbi Bejerano loved his people with a total, unqualified love. He would never willingly abandon his community. He was their teacher, their guide, their source of strength. Yet, he longed to live in the land of Israel. He dreamed of the day when he, his wife and their three children could fulfill the millennial Jewish prayer to dwell in the holy land and breathe its sacred air. But he had been born and raised in Tekirdag; his parents and many relatives were buried in the town's Jewish cemetery; the members of the community were his relatives, friends, students. His life was too intertwined with Tekirdag to simply pick up and leave. He was integral to the community, and they needed him. How could he possibly abandon them?

Yet, he could feel the winds of change. The "old timers" loved him, venerated him. But the Francophiles were growing in number and influence. Although they respected Rabbi Bejerano, they saw him increasingly as a relic of the past. Rabbi Bejerano sensed the incipient alienation.

Maurice Muscatel was the wealthiest Jew of Tekirdag. He used to be known as "Moshe" or "Mushon." Now he was Maurice. He rarely spoke in Judeo-Spanish, preferring to use his faulty French—which he pronounced with a Spanish accent. He saw himself as the avatar of modernity, of progress. He rarely raised his voice . . . but he rarely had to do so. Whenever he expressed an opinion, people invariably agreed. His wealth gave him power. He was the most generous supporter of the synagogue and other Jewish institutions. Who could risk antagonizing him by disagreeing with him? If he held back on his donations, the entire community would suffer.

Maurice Muscatel decided it was time for the Jewish community in Tekirdag to hire a rabbi with a modern outlook. Without asking anyone for advice or consent, he made discreet inquiries among his business associates in other towns; he learned of a young rabbi who had been trained in the schools of the Alliance Israelite Universelle, and who was therefore deeply steeped in French language and culture. This rabbi was said to be very bright, very fashionable, and very modern. For Maurice Muscatel, these were the ideal qualifications.

Again, without asking anyone for advice or consent, Maurice Muscatel contacted this young rabbi—Rene Tedeschi—and invited him to be rabbi of the Jews of Tekirdag. He offered Rabbi Tedeschi a generous salary, a house, and other benefits. The young rabbi was flattered and pleased; he could not refuse such a splendid opportunity.

Maurice Muscatel called a meeting of the leaders of the community and informed them that he had chosen a new rabbi for Tekirdag. He emphasized the many virtues of Rabbi Tedeschi, especially that he was a rising star with a growing reputation, and that his French culture would make him attractive to the new generation. No one among the community leaders stood up to ask any questions about Maurice Muscatel's choice—Who authorized him to search for a new rabbi? What right did he have to make a choice without first consulting the community's leadership? Did this new rabbi have an understanding of the culture and traditions of the Jews of Tekirdag? No one asked, although everyone thought about these questions. No one had the gumption to stand up to Maurice Muscatel. He was soft spoken, generous with his money, and relentless. Whatever he decided was not subject to discussion or debate.

So Rabbi Tedeschi came to Tekirdag with his wife and two young children. They moved into a large, expensive home provided by Maurice Muscatel. He drew a large salary, paid in full by Maurice Muscatel. Rabbi Tedeschi certainly realized that he was at the mercy of Maurice Muscatel, that his livelihood depended exclusively on this one rich man. He knew that he must satisfy Maurice Muscatel's wishes if he intended to remain in his plush new position.

Rabbi Bejerano had not been consulted about whether the community should engage a new rabbi or whether this particular rabbi was a suitable choice. Maurice Muscatel was in charge, not Rabbi Bejerano.

Rabbi Tedeschi spoke almost exclusively in French. To the old timers, he spoke in Judeo-Spanish; but he clearly tried to avoid speaking in the old language. He gave learned discourses that few, if any, understood. He often mentioned the important people he knew, or whom he had met over the years. He gave the air of someone who was quite content with himself, who viewed himself as a modern, influential intellectual.

Rabbi Tedeschi had no use for Rabbi Bejerano. He showed the older rabbi no honor, no respect. To him, Rabbi Bejerano was a vestige of a bygone era and was best left alone. When questions of community policy or Jewish law arose, Rabbi Tedeschi dealt with them on his own, never consulting Rabbi Bejerano.

Rabbi Bejerano was humble and quiet. He did not have a high opinion of Rabbi Tedeschi, and thought that the new rabbi would undermine the spiritual and communal life of the Jews of Tekirdag. But he kept his views to himself. He was, after all, not the community's official rabbi. Rabbi Bejerano continued teaching, ministering to those in need, answering questions brought to him by students and friends.

Rabbi Tedeschi sought to undermine Rabbi Bejerano's influence in every way possible. He forbade the older rabbi from teaching in the synagogue; he insisted that all halakhic questions be brought to him, not to Rabbi Bejerano; he scoffed at people who turned to Rabbi Bejerano for advice, friendship and support.

So Rabbi Bejerano's world became narrower and darker. But he was a pious man, and did not worry about his own feelings. He felt sad, though, that his beloved community was being dragged down by a pompous, egotistical young rabbi who seemed more interested in his own advancement than in the wellbeing of the community.

People in the community realized that their world was changing. Whereas Rabbi Bejerano was always there for them, Rabbi Tedeschi was rarely there for them. Whereas Rabbi Bejerano loved them, Rabbi Tedeschi had little patience with them. Whereas Rabbi Bejerano lived simply and asked no salary, Rabbi Tedeschi lived luxuriously and took a huge salary. Whereas Rabbi Bejerano radiated a beautiful, spiritual piety in the Judeo-Spanish tradition, Rabbi Tedeschi reflected a cold, calculated French aloofness.

But no one would stand up to Maurice Muscatel. People bowed their heads and accepted the new situation. If Maurice Muscatel wanted Rabbi Tedeschi, then Rabbi Tedeschi would be the town's rabbi. If Maurice Muscatel wanted to undermine Rabbi Bejerano's influence, then Rabbi Bejerano's impact would be undermined.

Rabbi Bejerano wondered why the community was so sheepish, why no one rose to question the choice of the new rabbi, why no one defended Rabbi Bejerano's religious worldview. But he was resigned to the new reality and was not bitter.

Now that the community increasingly seemed to function without him, Rabbi Bejerano began to consider seriously his goal of moving to the Holy Land. Emigrating to the land of Israel would entail a breach—probably an irreparable breach—with life in Tekirdag. And yet, these were new times and one could not live in the past. If Maurice Muscatel and Rabbi Tedeschi thought that the future of the Jews was in French, Rabbi Bejerano thought the Jewish future was in Hebrew in the ancient Jewish homeland.

A breaking point was reached on the first Sabbath after Passover. It was an age-old custom for the men of the community to gather that Shabbat afternoon in order to chant a chapter of the "Ethics of the Fathers" in Hebrew, and in Ladino translation. They sang one chapter each Shabbat afternoon, until the onset of the festival of Shavuoth. As usual, the men— including Rabbi Bejerano—met in the synagogue. Rabbi Tedeschi presided. As the men opened their booklets of "Ethics of the Fathers," Rabbi Tedeschi told them to put the pamphlets down. They were no longer going to follow the traditional chanting in Hebrew and Ladino, but he would give a lecture in French instead. When Rabbi Bejerano quietly objected, saying that it was not right to annul an age-old tradition, Rabbi Tedeschi sharply reprimanded him. "I am the rabbi here, not you. The old tradition is regressive. We need to move in a new direction." Rabbi Bejerano lowered his head. Maurice Muscatel beamed with pride. The men—all of whom would surely have preferred to follow the tradition— remained silent. So Rabbi Tedeschi gave a learned discourse in French, which no one except Maurice Muscatel wanted to hear.

When Rabbi Bejerano saw that the men—the people he had served and nurtured for so many years—did not stand up for the tradition or for his honor, he realized that the time to move to the land of Israel had come. Tekirdag was no longer Tekirdag; the community was no longer his community. His years of devotion and dedication no longer seemed to matter to anyone.

Within the next few months, Rabbi Bejerano closed his business, sold his home, and made the arrangements to move to the land of Israel. Although a deep residue of sadness imbued his soul, he was filled with happy anticipation at starting a new life. Turkish Jews in the land of Israel heard that he and family were relocating to the Holy Land, and they enthusiastically offered him a position as their rabbi in Bat Yam. Rabbi Bejerano gladly accepted, on condition that he would take no salary from the community. He would open a store in Bat Yam and earn his living from his business.

When the day of departure arrived, many members of the community came to see the Bejerano family off. All had tears in their eyes. The Bejeranos cried at leaving the town of their births, the town where generations of their family had lived and died. They were going to the Promised Land—but in some way, they felt they were going into exile. Members of the community cried because they knew they were losing the most spiritual, beautiful soul they had ever known. They knew that their own lives would be irreparably diminished by the departure of Rabbi Bejerano. The Midrash teaches: when a righteous person leaves a town, the town's glory and honor also leave with him.

Rabbi Bejerano's family settled in Bat Yam among the growing settlement of Turkish Jews there. They rejoiced in life in the Holy Land. They thrived in the Hebrew-speaking community, where people also loved to speak and hear Judeo-Spanish. But Rabbi Bejerano still ached for his home community in Tekirdag. He could still envision the people there, he could still hear the ghosts of the earlier generations. He lived in the land of Israel and loved the land of Israel; but he never overcame the feeling of also being in exile.

As could have been predicted by anyone other than Maurice Muscatel, the Jewish community of Tekirdag started to unravel. Rabbi Tedeschi was viewed as a self-serving, supercilious, pseudo-Frenchman. The old-timers missed the homey wisdom of Rabbi Bejerano and his sweet Judeo-Spanish. The younger, French-educated, members of the community were drifting away from religious tradition altogether, and Rabbi Tedeschi had little influence on them.

At first, a trickle of Jews moved away from Tekirdag. Some relocated in Bat Yam to be with Rabbi Bejerano. Many set out to create new lives for themselves in

America. The trickle soon grew into a steady stream. The traditionalists no longer felt comfortable in a Tekirdag without Rabbi Bejerano, a Tekirdag led by Muscatel and Tedeschi. The "progressives" found Tekirdag too small and too provincial. Their French education alienated them from the old ways of Jewish traditionalism. They moved to the more cosmopolitan Istanbul; or to Paris; or to other large cities around the world.

Rabbi Tedeschi quickly realized that he would not have a long future in Tekirdag. He did not want to be captain of a sinking ship and he did not have the capacity or the will to try to set the ship aright. So he discreetly put out feelers and found a new prestigious position in Alexandria, Egypt. Once everything was finalized, he informed Maurice Muscatel that he was moving to Alexandria.

Maurice Muscatel was outraged and said some nasty words to Rabbi Tedeschi. The rabbi smiled back wanly, and walked away with a self-confident, arrogant stride. He no longer was in the thrall of Maurice Muscatel.

Rabbi Bejerano had left Tekirdag. Rabbi Tedeschi was leaving Tekirdag. Dozens of Jewish families had left Tekirdag, with dozens more planning to move away. The traditionalists were downcast; the progressives were alienated; the synagogue was attended by fewer and fewer people.

Maurice Muscatel, the richest man in town, the leader with a soft voice and a progressive vision, was feeling increasingly angry. He was watching his community disintegrate right before his eyes. Why didn't the people realize that his decisions were the best decisions? Why had they forsaken him after all he had done for the community? He was right, wasn't he? He was rich and powerful, wasn't he? He had the best vision for the future of the Jews of Tekirdag, didn't he?

Maurice Muscatel was the avatar of progress for the Jewish community of Tekirdag.

MURDER

America.

That was the dream of so many poor Jews in the old Ottoman Empire at the beginning of the 20th century. America was hope, a chance for a better life, a way out of poverty and squalor, a bastion of freedom.

America.

Enthusiasm for the new "promised land" spread from heart to heart. Thousands of hopeful souls uprooted themselves from the old world and set sail for the new.

Among them, in 1908, were Bohor Yehuda Angel and his eldest son Moshe. They left the Island of Rhodes and made the long, arduous trip to Seattle, Washington, where a small community of Rhodes Jews had already settled.

Bohor Yehuda was a sturdy, pious man. He left his six young children in Rhodes with his wife Bulissa Esther. He and Moshe planned to work hard, earn money, and bring the entire family to Seattle as soon as possible.

Bohor Yehuda opened a shoe-shine stand in downtown Seattle. Moshe worked at various odd jobs. They lived simply and with great self-sacrifice.

They regularly sent money to their family in Rhodes to sustain them until they could save enough to bring them all to Seattle. It took them three years of toil and scrimping before they finally raised the necessary funds.

Bulissa Esther received the news with ineffable joy. The past three years had been difficult. Separation from a husband so many thousands of miles away in a strange land was not easy. Caring for six children in the absence of their father was a huge challenge. Although she was blessed with great wisdom and patience, Bulissa Esther was taxed to the limit of her abilities. At last, she could now arrange to travel with her children to America and the family could once again be united.

Bulissa Esther and her six children set sail in the summer of 1911. They traveled steerage, but no one complained. They were on their way to the freedom, happiness, and the promise of America. They were on their way to family reunion.

When they arrived in New York harbor, they looked forward to stepping onto American soil. They would soon take a train cross-country to Seattle. All would be well.

As they exited the ship, all passengers were brought to the immigration office. American officials checked their names, their places of origin, their ultimate destinations in the United States. They asked many questions, although most of the immigrants did not know English and could not understand what was being asked of them. Somehow, though, most of the passengers answered well enough and received papers admitting them into the United States.

When the turn of Bulissa Esther and her six children came, she stood before the examining officers with trembling anticipation. She told the officials that they were on their way to Seattle to reunite with her husband and eldest son.

One of the officials, following standard immigration procedures, checked the family members to determine if they had any obvious diseases or health issues that would prohibit their entry into the United States. Bulissa Esther and five of her children were deemed to be healthy. Her nine-year-old son, Joseph, was found to have a scalp disease, tinias. This was not a serious health problem in itself; but the immigration official ruled that Joseph could not be admitted into the country due to his disease.

Bulissa Esther's heart jumped a beat when she was made to understand that Joseph could not enter the United States. She broke down crying. She pleaded with the officials. He is just a little boy, we will get medicine for his tinias, please let him in, what am I to do if you do not admit him? We've waited three years for my husband and son to raise the funds to bring us here! We can't go back to Rhodes again!

No, said the official, you don't have to go back to Rhodes. You and five of your children can continue your trip to Seattle. But Joseph can't be admitted into the United States.

Please, have mercy on a mother and her children.

Have mercy on a nine year old boy. How can we separate him from the rest of us? How will he go back to Rhodes alone? Who will care for him there?

That is not our problem, said the official. Joseph cannot be admitted. You need to decide what to do now.

America.

The promised land. A land with laws, but without mercy. A land that would turn a young boy away, that would break the hearts of a good, honest family.

Bulissa Esther was beside herself with grief. She could not bring her family back to Rhodes. But neither could she abandon little Joseph.

As it happened, a Jewish man from Rhodes, who had been on the same ship as Bulissa Esther, was also denied entry into the United States due to a health problem. He had no choice but to return to Rhodes. When he heard Bulissa Esther crying, he came over to her and learned of the problem with Joseph. He volunteered to bring Joseph back to Rhodes with him, to settle him in with a family of relatives until such time as Bohor Yehuda could raise enough money to pay passage for Joseph to join the family in Seattle.

Bulissa Esther had no other realistic option. She thanked the man profusely for agreeing to look after Joseph. So she kissed her beloved son and said goodbye. All the brothers and sisters hugged Joseph and promised that they would see him again soon.

Bulissa Esther and five of her children traveled on

to Seattle, reunited with Bohor Yehuda and Moshe, and gradually adapted to their new lives in America. Joseph was brought to the home of relatives in Rhodes. Bulissa Esther prayed for the day when Joseph could be brought together with the rest of the family in Seattle.

That day never came.

Bohor Yehuda could scarcely earn enough to support his large family in Seattle, let alone to save money to buy passage for Joseph. Meanwhile, world events were impacting on life in Rhodes, making Joseph's travel to the United States increasingly unlikely.

War broke out between Italy and Turkey, with Italian forces occupying the Island of Rhodes in May 1912. After nearly four centuries of Turkish dominion, Rhodes was now under Italian control. Italy was officially granted Rhodes in July 1923 under the Treaty of Lausanne. The Jews of Rhodes, along with the other residents of the island, soon began to speak Italian, to think Italian, to be Italian subjects. Economic life in Rhodes blossomed. Little Joseph grew up at a time of growing optimism among the Jews of Rhodes.

He couldn't easily travel to America during the Turco-Italian War years. Then World War I broke out in July 1914, making travel across the Atlantic Ocean dangerous if not impossible. By the time the war ended in November 1918, Joseph was a young man, already comfortable in his life in Italian-ruled Rhodes. In due course, he was married to a lovely wife,

Sinyorou; and they went on to have four children—two boys and two girls. Life was moving along well. They could see no reason to move to America; and in any case, American quota laws of 1921 and 1924 dramatically limited the number of immigrants eligible to enter the United States. Joseph had been turned away from America once; he had no desire to face American immigration officials a second time.

But conditions in Rhodes were to change radically. In June 1936, Italy aligned itself with Nazi Germany. Jews living in Italian territories—like Jews living in Germany—became victims of a horrific policy of anti-Semitism. The Jews of Rhodes were thunderstruck by the dramatic undermining of their lives and their livelihoods. The Rabbinical College of Rhodes was forced to close. Jews in Rhodes were required to keep their stores open on the Jewish Sabbath and festivals. In September 1938, anti-Jewish laws went into effect in Rhodes that prohibited kosher slaughter of animals. Jews were no longer allowed to buy property, employ non-Jewish servants, send their children to government schools. Non-Jews were forbidden from patronizing Jewish doctors or pharmacists. Jews who had settled in Rhodes after January 1919 were expelled from the Island. (They were the fortunate ones!)

For a short period in the early 1940s, there was a slight easing of the anti-Jewish measures. Yet, conditions were dire. Aside from dealing with their loss of civil status and human dignity, they had to deal with the ongoing hardships of living in a war zone. British planes dropped bombs on Rhodes in their effort to defeat the Axis powers, and dozens of Jews were among those killed in these attacks.

When Mussolini was removed from power in July 1943, the Jews of Rhodes thought their troubles were over. But contrary to their expectations, the Germans occupied Rhodes. The situation of the Jews worsened precipitously. In July 1944, the Jews of Rhodes had all their valuables confiscated by the Germans. They were then crowded into three small freight ships. Of the nearly 1,700 Rhodes Jews deported by the Nazis, only 151 survived. Almost all the Jews of Rhodes were viciously murdered in Auschwitz.

Among those who suffered this cruel and inhuman death were the entire family of Joseph Angel.

Little did the American immigration official realize in 1911, that by turning away a little boy with a scalp infection, he was condemning that boy and family to a calamitous destruction. That official no doubt slept peacefully the night he sent Joseph back to Rhodes, separating the young son from his mother and siblings. The official was following the rules.

If that official was still alive in July 1944, he probably slept the sleep of the innocent, not realizing that his actions led to the death of an entire family. His dreams were not haunted by nightmares of the ghosts of Joseph's family.

THE TRAIN

LUZ ALVAREZ woke up once again with memories of her troubling dream. For the past few months, almost every night, she had the same dream. She was on a train—but it was the wrong train!

Luz was not a mystic. She did not believe in prophecies through dreams. And yet, she wondered why this same dream recurred so often.

From all appearances, she was a happy woman. She was married to a loving husband; they had three lovely children, ranging in age from six to twelve years old. They lived in a nice home. They were model citizens in their community in Santa Fe. They had a nice circle of friends, they were doing fine financially, they were healthy.

Luz had always felt that she was on the right train.

When she related her dream to her husband, he reassured her that dreams are merely figments of imagination, illusions. This dream would go away soon enough. Perhaps the dream reflected a typical mid-life crisis, the classic angst that so many people face when they hit their late 30s or early 40s.

But Luz was not so sure. This dream was seeping deeper and deeper into her life; she was trying with all her might to unravel its message. The more she thought about it, though, the more she felt herself to be on a train going to the wrong destination. This was no illusion or mid-life crisis. This was something deep and serious and very real.

She confided in her priest; but he only told her to pray more devoutly and to let the Lord cleanse her of her bad thoughts. She went to a psychiatrist; but he was of no help in deciphering the dream. In desperation, she went to one of the Native American healers, an elderly woman with mysterious eyes. This woman spoke rhythmically, softly, wisely.

"If you keep dreaming that you are on the wrong train—then you are on the wrong train! So you now need to get on the right train. Think where you are headed; think where you need to reach. But more importantly, think of where you entered the train in the first place. Go back to the beginning of your trip and then you might discover your error in getting on the wrong train."

Luz asked: "But where will I find the right train?"

The wise woman replied: "You will find the right train once you know where your trip began."

For the next days and weeks, Luz scoured her memories of the past. Where indeed did she board the train? Where was she intending to go?

By chance, or not by chance, she read a small item in the newspaper announcing a lecture to be given by a rabbi of Spanish descent at the local synagogue. The topic: "The Anousim of the American Southwest: Searching for the Roots of Spanish Crypto-Jews."

Ordinarily, this topic would have no interest whatever for her. She was a Catholic. She had no connection with the Jews—or the descendants of crypto-Jews—who lived in her town. But, by chance or not by chance, she decided to attend the lecture.

For the first time in her life, she learned of the forced conversion of Jews in Spain during the 14th and 15th centuries. She learned of the expulsion of Jews from Spain in 1492. She learned of Jews who converted to Catholicism under duress and who maintained their Jewishness in secret. These crypto-Jews were hunted and haunted by the agents of the unspeakable cruelties of the Spanish and Portuguese Inquisitions. The Catholic monarchs and the Catholic church—in the name of God— inflicted terrible horrors, tortures, exile and death on hundreds of thousands of Jews.

Luz learned of tormented crypto-Jews who fled the Iberian Peninsula in search of safety and freedom. Among them were those who settled in the New World, thinking themselves far away from the vicious arms of the Inquisition. But the Inquisition came to the New World. The crypto-Jews of New Spain (Mexico) went deeper into hiding. Some moved northward into the American Southwest. After many generations, after almost every vestige of Jewishness had been lost, some of the descendants of crypto-Jews—known in Hebrew as *benei Anousim* (descendants of the forced ones)—were now finding and reclaiming their Jewish roots.

As the rabbi spoke to several hundred listeners,

Luz felt a remarkable spiritual energy filling the synagogue. It seemed to her that most members of the audience were themselves of crypto-Jewish background. As they listened to the rabbi's words, pieces in the puzzle of their lives were starting to come together.

The thought flashed through Luz's mind: am I one of these people? Were my ancestors Spanish Jews who had been forcibly converted by a triumphalist Catholic church? She had never heard a whisper of such a thing from her parents or relatives; but might they themselves not have known of their Jewish roots?

Toward the end of his speech, the rabbi commented on various practices that crypto-Jews had observed over the generations. Some lit candles in basements on Friday nights. Some sat on the floor when they mourned the passing of a loved one. Some only ate meat after it had first been soaked and salted to remove its blood. Most had no idea that these were vestiges of their family's Jewishness.

The rabbi then mentioned another practice. Some descendants of crypto-Jews did not sweep dust through the doorways leading to the outside of their houses. Rather, they gathered the dust into a pile, swept it neatly into a paper, and then carried it out of their houses. This, explained the rabbi, was a vestige of a practice of medieval Spanish Jews. According to Jewish tradition, a *mezuzah* is affixed to the doorpost of the house. The *mezuzah* contains a parchment with passages from the Torah. Spanish Jews felt it would disgrace the holiness of the *mezuzah* if they were to sweep dirt through the doorway. So they were careful to sweep the dirt inside the house, and then carry it out of the house in a respectful manner.

Luz felt her heart jump. This is exactly what her mother had done when she swept. Luz had asked her mother many times why she didn't just sweep the dirt out the door, and her mother had always answered: "because this is how we do it."

After the lecture, Luz returned home as in a dream.

And her nightmares about being on the wrong train stopped.

During the following months, she engaged in frenzied genealogical research. She interviewed elder relatives. She read histories of the Spanish Jews. She networked with descendants of crypto-Jews. She started to study the teachings of Judaism. Her passion for things Jewish became an obsession that engulfed her life and plunged her family into discord.

Her husband was a faithful Catholic. He resented his wife's deepening connection with Judaism. He feared that her new-found Jewishness would adversely affect their children. Already, she was telling them that they really were Jews, that their ancestors had been tortured by the Catholic Inquisition. She wanted her children to join her as they all reclaimed their Jewish heritage. She wanted her husband to join in this spiritual adventure and transformation. But he was not comfortable with this.

Luz no longer attended the Catholic church nor observed Catholic religious rites. She wanted her children to be enrolled in Jewish religious school rather than the Sunday School of the church. Eventually, her husband gave in. He wanted to save the marriage and maintain his family. If Luz and the children were going through a "Jewish phase," he would be patient with them.

Luz joined the synagogue and attended services regularly with her children. She observed more and more of the Jewish religion, including transforming her kitchen into a kosher kitchen. She felt and understood that she was now back on the right train. Her life made sense. She had re-connected with her origins, reclaimed her rightful Jewish heritage. She knew where she began, and she knew her destination. She would live and die as a Jew. She would fulfill the dreams and aspirations of ancestors who had been forcibly torn from their religion and their people. She would hear their voices and be their mouthpiece.

As Luz found great peace and inner strength, so too did her children draw on her inspiration. They were feeling themselves to be Jewish.

Then, one night, Luz's husband had a nightmare. The nightmare recurred night after night. He dreamt that he was on a train. But it was the wrong train.

AND THOUGH HE TARRY

FROM THE MOMENT Uriel Nasi began to attend synagoguge services at Congregation Ohavei Shalom, the tranquility of the worshipers was shattered. This newcomer ruined everything.

Uriel Nasi was a huge man—about six feet five inches tall, weighing at least 350 pounds. The immense weight of his body was concentrated in the section below his heart and above his waist, so that this mass of fat jutted out in an unpleasant, aggressive manner. His posture was impeccable, making his belly all the more menacing. He sported a scraggly gray goatee, but dyed the thin layer of hair atop his head a vulgar shade of orange. If he thought this made him appear younger or more attractive, he was sadly mistaken.

He carried himself in the arrogant, self-righteous style reserved for the most obnoxious snoots; he sneered at others, and went out of his way to show his contempt for them. He rarely spoke to anyone. From his towering height, he looked down and disapprovingly at his fellow congregants. He gave the impression of wanting to be anywhere but with them, but that he unfortunately had no choice but to pray with them because there was no other synagogue near by.

Uriel Nasi did not conform to the congregation's long held practices. He stood when the custom was to be seated; he sat when the custom was to stand. He prayed in a loud voice, usually some pages ahead or behind the congregation, so as to confuse them in their prayers. He sang the prayers to his own tunes at his own key, with no regard for the synagogue's traditions.

He called attention to his conspicuous piety by draping his prayer shawl over his head, even though no one else in the congregation—not even the rabbi—did so. During the reader's repetition of the silent prayer, he noisily removed his *tefillin* and replaced them with a second set of *tefillin* in keeping with the ruling of Rabbeinu Tam. No one else in the congregation—not even the rabbi—followed this stringent practice. But Uriel Nasi wanted it to be known that he was exceedingly pious, meticulous in all matters of Jewish law down to the most minute detail.

The rabbi of Congregation Ohavei Shalom—Aharon Cohen—was a wise but timid soul who detested controversy and confrontation. He was polite to Uriel Nasi, even though the latter did not reciprocate the courtesy. Rabbi Cohen was perceptive enough to recognize that the newcomer was disrupting the congregation, but timid enough to pretend not to notice the grumblings of the congregants.

One by one, men stopped attending morning

services. They preferred to pray at home without a quorum, rather than come to synagogue where they would be agitated by the arrogance and bombastic behavior of Uriel Nasi. The morning *minyan* was on the verge of dissolution.

Realizing that he needed to do something, Rabbi Cohen spoke softly with Uriel Nasi, suggesting that it would be nice if he chanted his prayers more quietly, if he would sit and stand according to the practice of the congregation. Uriel Nasi jutted out his belly, looked disgustedly at the rabbi, and did not even offer a word of response. He simply continued with his accustomed practices, without giving the least heed to the rabbi's requests.

A committee of disgruntled congregants demanded to meet with Rabbi Cohen. The rabbi put off this meeting as long as he could, but finally had to give in. The meeting was held in his office one morning after prayer services.

"I suggest that we ban Mr. Nasi from the synagogue," said one congregant. "He is unpleasant, rude, and disruptive. When I come to synagogue, I want to pray in peace and quiet, as was the case before Mr. Nasi started to attend. Now, each morning I leave the synagogue unhappy, nervous and angry."

"The problem is: Nasi is alienating our members," said another congregant. "People are dropping out of the *minyan*. People may start their own separate *minyan*, and our synagogue will lose members and support. Why should we allow this stranger to undermine the wellbeing of Ohavei Shalom?"

"I feel that we are being abused," added another congregant. "We come to synagogue in good faith to say our prayers—and we are treated abusively. Why should we have to put up with this insolence?"

Rabbi Cohen listened sadly as the stream of complaints continued. At last, it was his turn to speak. He bowed his head, shrugged his shoulders, raised his eyebrows. "Yes, yes," he said, "I know we have a problem. I've tried speaking with Uriel, but he does not listen to my suggestions. Yes, he does appear arrogant and unpleasant, and yes, he is noisy and disruptive. But here is my question: is it right to ban a Jew from praying in our synagogue? He is, after all, a religiously observant man; he comes to prayers faithfully each morning. Do we have the moral and religious permission to prevent him from praying with a *minyan?*"

The committee members were deeply disappointed with Rabbi Cohen's comments. "Yes," they said with one voice, "yes, we do have the moral right and responsibility to prevent a disruptive person from praying in our synagogue. Why should he have the right to pray in such a manner that drives the rest of us away?"

Rabbi Cohen lowered his eyes. He detested having to make decisions, especially decisions that involved unpleasantness. He realized, though, that his congregants raised valid points. Unless Uriel Cohen could be controlled or removed, the very future of the synagogue was at risk. Rabbi Cohen's own job was at risk.

"I shall speak to him again," said Rabbi Cohen in a soft voice. "I shall speak to him after services tomorrow morning." The meeting ended; the problem would be resolved tomorrow morning once and for all.

The next morning, Rabbi Cohen arrived at the synagogue with a frightened heart and trembling hands. He knew he must confront Uriel Nasi, but he dreaded the confrontation. What if Nasi rejected the rabbi's comments? What if he shouted unpleasant words at the rabbi?

Amazingly, perhaps by Divine Providence, Uriel Nasi did not show up for prayers that morning. Rabbi Cohen was infinitely relieved that the feared confrontation could be put off another day. Congregants were edgy and annoyed; they had hoped to have the problem solved this morning, and now it would need to drag on another day.

The next morning, Uriel Nasi did not attend services. Nor the next morning, nor the morning after that. What happened to him? Where was he? Nobody knew. Nasi vanished as suddenly as he had originally turned up at the synagogue some months earlier. A week passed, two weeks passed . . . no Uriel Nasi. Rabbi Cohen was profoundly grateful that the problem had solved itself. The congregants gradually re-adjusted to life without Uriel Nasi at morning services. The *minyan* filled up again with the men who had refused to pray at the synagogue as long as Uriel Nasi was engaging in his antics. Now there was peace and tranquility at Congregation

Ohavei Shalom. The noisy trouble maker had left.

Everyone was happy, but not completely happy. Something was missing at morning prayers, something vague and undefined. The prayers were chanted as usual; all the customs were observed as usual; Uriel Nasi was not there to disrupt or annoy anyone. Yet, something was missing in the spirit of the congregation. Things somehow did not seem altogether in order.

One morning after services, one of the congregants said: "You know, we certainly are lucky that Uriel Nasi doesn't disrupt our services any more."

Another congregant chimed in: "Yes, we certainly are better off now; we can pray in peace and quiet as we used to do before he showed up in synagogue."

A third congregant said: "We are well rid of him. He was arrogant, insufferable."

A moment of silence ensued. Then one congregant said: "Yes, but I actually think that I miss him! He was comical, he added a certain eccentric charm to our *minyan*."

Another moment of silence ensued. Then, one by one, congregants shared their reminiscences of Uriel Nasi. He was obnoxious—but pious. He was rude—and yet, he had a certain aristocratic air about him. He was noisy—and yet, he actually had a pleasant singing voice. One by one, congregants expressed words of appreciation for the man who had almost caused the dissolution of the congregation.

A spirit of remorse entered the hearts of the

congregants. Perhaps we should have been nicer to him, perhaps we should have demonstrated kindliness toward the stranger. Maybe it was our own fault that things deteriorated; we should have been more compassionate, more respectful of his feelings. Maybe he would have behaved better if we ourselves had treated him more lovingly.

Rabbi Cohen listened to the conversation, and finally found the courage to speak: "I had told you that it wasn't right for us to ban a Jew from the synagogue."

"We didn't have to ban him," they reminded the rabbi. "He disappeared on his own."

"Yes, but maybe he stopped coming to synagogue because he sensed our hostility."

People were filled with sadness and regret. As they left the synagogue that morning, Rabbi Cohen commented dolefully: "Perhaps Uriel Nasi was really Elijah the Prophet in disguise. Maybe he came here to test us. Maybe if we had been nicer, we would have been blessed by Elijah and would have proven worthy to receive the long-awaited Messiah."

Day after day, people attended services and looked to see if Uriel Nasi had returned. Week after week, month after month, year after year—the people waited and hoped.

Uriel Nasi never returned to Congregation Ohavei Shalom.

THE TAKEOVER

"WE ARE HERE to serve the clients. If we work for them with integrity and skill, they trust us. They even like us. When the clients are well-served, we make our money honestly. Everyone is happy, the company does well, the clients do well . . . but the key is: we work for the clients, they don't work for us."

So spoke Salvador Russo, the founder and outgoing chairman of the board of the Russo Investment Company based in New York City with offices in the Wall Street district. Salvador Russo was a handsome man of seventy-five. He was as healthy and robust as a forty-year-old, full of energy, new ideas, and forward-looking plans. He played tennis every morning, he kept a busy social schedule . . . he was—at age seventy-five—in the prime of life. And he was quite wealthy. He and his wife traveled widely and frequently. They had a mansion in the Hamptons; and apartments in the best neighborhoods of Jerusalem, Paris and London.

Salvador Russo was an American success story. His parents had emigrated to the United States from Salonika in 1913. They were penniless Sephardic Jews who came to start a new life in the land of the free.

Salvador's father was a barber who scarcely earned enough to support his wife and six children. But in spite of their poverty, they were a happy and dignified family. The elder Russo stressed the importance of punctuality, neatness and good manners. Salvador learned these values well.

During World War II, Salvador enlisted in the United States Army and served in Europe. He distinguished himself in combat and won a medal of honor for his courage in saving the lives of fellow soldiers who were badly wounded in battle. He was sturdy, strong and reliable. Officers and fellow soldiers respected him . . . and liked him.

After the war, he returned to New York. As a veteran, he was able to attend Columbia College at the government's expense. He was a diligent student. While he excelled in the liberal arts, his true gift was in economics and finance. He was twenty-five when he earned his B.A. from Columbia, *summa cum laude.* Shortly after graduation, he was married to Regina Mutal, a childhood sweetheart whose family also had roots in Salonika.

Instead of looking for employment in existing firms, Salvador founded his own investment company. He started off with little capital, no experience, and no clients. He emptied his savings account in order to pay rent for a small office in downtown New York. He was not afraid to take risks; he had the calm confidence of a winner.

After a year or two of struggling, he started to see his company grow. His remarkable affability won him friends . . . and clients. His hugely successful investments won him admiration and gratitude, and more clients. By the firm's tenth anniversary, it was already a financial powerhouse and Salvador Russo was a rich man. By the firm's fiftieth anniversary, he was retiring as chairman of the board, and planned to devote his remaining years to philanthropic projects in the United States and Israel.

Once he had decided to retire, he wanted to be sure that the firm was passed into good hands. His only son, Robert, had no interest in business. He grew up in a wealthy home and had enough money from his father, so that he never had to go to work. He viewed himself as a poet, and found a job teaching literature at Portland State University in Oregon. Salvador's two daughters were not inclined to go into their father's business, and Salvador's sons-in-law were equally uninterested in the business. Salvador faced the fact that the Russo Investment Company would not be led by a member of the Russo family.

So who would take over as chairman of this thriving and successful enterprise? There were many potential candidates!

Among the possibilities were several top officers of the Russo Investment Company. They knew the firm inside and out; they knew the clients; they understood the culture of the firm. They were competent, efficient, prompt and neat. Although Salvador thought highly enough of them to have hired them and elevated them in the firm, he was not sure about who would be the most able successor. After some months of agonizing over this issue, Salvador decided that he would hand over the chairmanship to David Barocas, a fellow Sephardic Jew, who was Vice President of Russo Investment Company, and who had been with the firm for twenty years. Although Barocas did not have the strength of character and *savoir faire* of Salvador, he would be a suitable head of the company and would maintain the high standards that Salvador had set during his tenure. He determined to present the candidacy of David Barocas at the next meeting of the company's board of directors. He assumed that his recommendation would be readily approved. Barocas would take over as chairman, and Salvador would go on with his active and productive life outside the precincts of the Russo Investment Company.

Although Salvador had always kept a very close eye on operations within the company, he was totally oblivious of the fact that an insurrection was quietly brewing on the company's board. One of the board members, Joe Lyons, had his own idea of who should be the next chairman of the board. Joe, being almost seventy years old, did not want the job himself; but he certainly did not want Barocas to have it either. Rather, he had his eyes on a candidate who was vice-chair of a competing company. He wanted to lure that man—Timothy Burbank—into the top position of the Russo Investment Company.

Lyons secretly lobbied members of the board, and pushed the candidacy of Burbank. He cajoled and even bribed fellow board members to see things his way. Burbank was new blood. Burbank was frequently quoted in the Wall Street Journal, Forbes, television business news channels and other media. He would pump new life into Russo Investment Company, a company—Lyons complained—that was going stale. By the time the board meeting was held, Lyons had lined up a majority of votes for Burbank, without Russo or Barocas realizing what had happened.

Salvador Russo addressed the fifteen members of the board, reviewing the great history of the firm, its dedication to its clients, its outstanding success in managing money. He spoke with pride of how he had opened the firm fifty years ago with no capital, and how he had led the company to become one of the powerful and respected investment companies in New York. He officially announced his retirement, indicating that he was ready to transition into a new and different phase of life.

He then informed the board of his choice of David Barocas to succeed him as chairman of the board. He spoke of Barocas's loyalty to the firm, his excellent investment skills, his commitment to neatness, punctuality and good manners. Most of all, he praised Barocas's commitment to clients. He viewed them—as Russo himself did—as friends, as an extended family. He expected board members to applaud the decision and vote Barocas in unanimously.

But Joe Lyons's hand went up, and he requested

the opportunity to speak.

"Salvador, we all appreciate your tremendous leadership over all these years. We congratulate you on your forthcoming retirement and wish you well. Before we vote on your successor, though, I would like to suggest an alternative candidate for this position. David Barocas is, of course, a trusted and capable man; but I think we need to move the firm in a different direction.

I would like the board to consider the candidacy of Timothy Burbank. I have spoken confidentially with Timothy and I believe he would be willing to take this position if it were offered to him."

Salvador Russo was stunned but not ruffled. Remaining calm and poised, he interrupted Lyons's speech. "Thank you, Joe, for putting another name on the table for our consideration. I am surprised, though, that you hadn't discussed this with me previously. This is obviously embarrassing for me and for David, and I suspect that the other members of the board are also uncomfortable. Perhaps we should defer our decision until such time as we all have a chance to discuss this matter more carefully among ourselves."

"No," said Joe Lyons, with a snake-like smile on his thin face. "We should make a decision at this meeting." Lyons knew he had enough votes to win. He did not want to postpone the vote since that would give Russo time to do his own lobbying among board members.

"What is the pleasure of the board?" asked Russo.

The board voted, and it was eight to seven to make the decision now, at this meeting.

Salvador Russo sensed that he had been out-maneuvered, something that had never happened to him before. Well, he thought, once a lion has been de-fanged, the little hyenas get arrogant. They know I'm leaving, so they no longer fear me.

Salvador spoke: "Everyone here knows that I have always run this company democratically and have respected majority opinion on our board. I could have imposed my will as founder and major stakeholder in the firm . . . but I have not done so. I wanted—and want—this firm to be run honestly and fairly according to the best judgment of the board. So although I'm very disappointed in the outcome of this vote, I will abide by it. Joe, tell us why you think Timothy Burbank deserves to become chairman of the board of Russo Investment Company."

Lyons coughed smugly to clear his throat, and then made his case. "Salvador, this isn't about you but about the future of the company. You've served long and well; but we're at a crossroads now. There's a lot more competition out there. Our client base is getting older and we haven't been getting enough new, younger clients. Following the old ways won't work any longer.

Timothy Burbank is the right choice for us because he is a 'name,' a personality who will attract new business. People have heard of him, he is talked about in the news. When the public learns that he is chairman of Russo Investment Company, they'll be impressed; they'll open accounts with us.

If we care about the future of our company, we need to have a leader who will bring us to the next level and will expand our reputation. He is a public figure and that's what we need in order to grow.

We all know and respect David Barocas. He is a good man and certainly has been devoted to the firm for many years. But he—please forgive me David—lacks pizzazz; he's too mainstream, too boringly Wall Street. He'll maintain the status quo, and we'll keep losing market share to more aggressive companies.

At this juncture, we would be best served by offering the position of chairman of the board to Timothy Burbank."

Joe Lyons finished his presentation with a contented look on his face. He was confident of victory, his one and only victory over Salvador since he joined the Russo Investment Company twenty-five years before.

There was a nervous hush in the room. Salvador Russo waited a minute, and then offered his response:

"Timothy Burbank is the absolute wrong choice for our company. On a scale of one to ten, he is zero. He is not relevant to us and should not even be considered as a candidate for chairman of our company.

I've been in this business for 50 years. I know the

business well, and I know the players in the field. Timothy Burbank is an egomaniac who spends most of his energy trying to get his name into the newspapers or getting his unpleasant face in front of a television camera. He is a showman and an opportunist. He would be glad to have a plum position with our firm at a high salary . . . and he would stay here just until he could scare up a better offer from some other foolish company. He has a history of jumping from company to company.

It's not just that he lacks the basic virtues of neatness, promptness, efficiency, and good manners. It's that he always puts himself first, and couldn't care less about clients except insofar as they are the ones who provide him with his income.

His actual track record as an investor is not remarkably good. People are better off buying CDs at low rates of return rather than trusting Burbank with their money. Those who look at the data rather than at the P.R. glitz know that Timothy Burbank is a self-serving phony. He talks big, pretends to be a mover and shaker; but if you blow away the fluff, there's nothing left.

He does not—and never will—fit into the business culture of the Russo Investment Company. He has a reputation of being notoriously absent from his office; of never promptly returning calls or emails; of tardy attendance at meetings; of slovenly personal habits. We are a top notch elegant firm, he is a low class money grubber.

It would be irresponsible and foolish of this board

to offer the chairmanship to Burbank, a person of dubious character with a mediocre record of investment returns. We are fortunate in having among our own ranks a person of the quality of David Barocas. David puts clients first. David is capable, efficient and elegant. David's investment record is outstanding, and everyone in the business knows he is a solid, dependable and able money manager.

I ask the Board to elect David Barocas as chairman of the Russo Investment Company."

The vote was called. Timothy Burbank was elected by a majority of eight to seven.

Salvador Russo had never imagined that his career with the company would come to this conclusion. It was beyond belief that things had slipped away from him, that a slimy person like Joe Lyons could win over the majority of the board to oppose him. But it happened. The company that he built from scratch, that he had led for fifty solid years, had now turned against him and betrayed him.

After the meeting Salvador returned to his office together with David Barocas. Both were upset and humiliated. Salvador was ashamed that he had not been able to prevail with the board on David's behalf. David was ashamed that eight members of the board—whom he had considered as his friends—had voted against him. What now?

Salvador's genius was to take the long view of things, and not get bogged down or defeated by temporary setbacks. As he sat behind his desk, he leaned back, closed his eyes, and spoke softly.

"David, this was a bad day for us and a very bad day for the Russo Investment Company. But it's not the end of the world. We both have made very good money here, and neither of us will starve. I'm retiring from the company, that's already been established. I suspect that you will resign from the company, not wanting to remain among those who have betrayed you.

So here's what I'm thinking. Let's pull out all our own money from the company. Let's start a new company with you as chairman and me as senior investment advisor. Let's inform our clients of our new business. Those who wish to transfer their accounts to us, great. Those who want to leave their money here, that's their problem. We can name the new firm David Barocas Investments if you wish. I'll be there with my account and my advice; but I won't get in your way. It's all yours. I suspect that a few of the best people in the Russo Investment Company will want to come along with us. The world hasn't come to an end. This is an opportunity for a new beginning."

Within a year, David Barocas Investments opened its office, with Salvador Russo as the largest client. Some clients from the old firm transferred their accounts, but most others remained with the Russo Investment Company. Within two years, David Barocas Investments was doing quite well, with a much stronger return for its clients than the older firm.

Within a year, Timothy Burbank got his name in the newspaper dozens of times; appeared on five television news programs; was interviewed on radio frequently. He attended many parties and charity events, generally arriving late and generally drinking more than was good for him. He told many jokes and made people laugh. He wasn't too faithful about being in his office every day, and he was rarely if ever on time for meetings or appointments. But he told jokes, seemed successful, had lots of news coverage—he was a "name," a "star."

Within two years, morale at the Russo Investment Company had declined precipitously. The board members who had voted for Burbank were realizing the gravity of their mistake. The board members who had voted for Barocas had found new jobs elsewhere, including at David Barocas Investments. The old clients were increasingly unhappy with the poor returns on their investments. They missed Salvador's friendship and guidance. As for new clients, few ever actually materialized. Burbank didn't seem to mind, though. He was pulling in a huge salary, enjoying his fame, and keeping his eye open for a new and better opportunity.

Joe Lyons convinced Burbank to have the firm's name changed to Cutting Edge Investments Corporation, but the company's income declined. Its best personnel defected to other companies that were better managed. One by one, clients left the firm.

Salvador Russo might have become bitter and

angry at this ugly turn of events. The firm he had started, that had his name attached to it for over fifty years, had betrayed and repudiated him. That company, with its new name, was being led by an egotistical, self-serving joker who managed to advance himself in spite of his poor character and even worse investment record.

Salvador knew he could not save the situation. Life goes on. Let people live with the consequences of their decisions.

But Salvador was not bitter or angry beyond the first few months of leaving his office at the Russo Investment Company. He was a rich man with a full life. He did not need the Russo Investment Company for anything. He was glad to have helped his loyal friend, David Barocas, open his own investment company; and David was doing well.

Joe Lyons was glad that he had won a great victory by bringing Timothy Burbank on board as chairman of Russo's former company. When Lyons realized, though, that the Cutting Edge Investments Corporation was not doing too well, he decided to bail out and take his retirement. He had no intention of going down with a sinking ship, so he finagled a generous retirement package for himself, bestowed upon him through the courtesy of Timothy Burbank.

Burbank himself laughed all the way to the bank.

THE GOLD KEY

AT AGE SIXTY, Mort Barbanel looked back on his life and was not sure what to think.

Born in Salonika in 1923, he was among the nearly 60,000 Salonikan Jews deported by the Nazis in 1943. Almost all of these Jews were murdered in concentration camps. Mort's family and friends perished in the ovens of Auschwitz and other death camps, leaving him and the seventeen-hundred or so Salonikan Jewish survivors as a generation of orphans.

From the moment of the deportation, Mort determined that he would survive. He was healthy and athletic, a star soccer player. He felt in his bones that no matter what happened to everyone else, he was strong enough to survive. And he did survive long months of hard labor, nightmarish deprivation of food, shelter, medical care, and elementary human kindness. He survived even as he knew that millions of others were gassed to death and shoveled into the crematoria.

Throughout the agonies of his slave labor, he kept in mind two goals: to retrieve his family's past, and to create his family's future.

He was a descendant of the famed Don Yitzhak

Abarbanel, the great scholar and statesman who was the most famous figure among the Jews expelled from Spain in 1492. Before the expulsion, Abarbanel had been a high government official with close ties to King Ferdinand and Queen Isabella. The Spanish monarchs were keen on getting Abarbanel to convert to Catholicism so that he would not have to leave Spain, and so that his brilliant service to the Crown could continue unabated. But Don Yitzhak was a proud and noble Jew; he strove unsuccessfully to have the Edict of Expulsion rescinded. When the date of expulsion arrived, Don Yitzhak was among the many thousands of Spanish Jews who left their homes in Spain, maintaining their staunch Jewish faith rather than accepting baptism.

The Abarbanels traced their family's origin to King David. They were nobility. They were the aristocracy of the Jewish people. A popular Judeo-Spanish proverb boasted: *"Basta mi nombre que es Abarbanel."* My name is enough; it is Abarbanel. That name carried tremendous history and tremendous honor.

According to family tradition, Don Yitzhak brought with him a gold key which had opened the door to his palatial home in Spain. This heirloom was a symbol of golden times past and a hope for golden days yet to come. The gold key was passed down through the generations of Don Yitzhak's descendants and had come into the possession of Mort Barbanel's father, Yehudah, in Salonika. When the Nazis entered the city in 1943, Yehudah feared the worst; he took his most valuable possessions—including the gold key—and buried them deep in the earth under the tiles of his home's courtyard. He then showed his family members where he had buried these things.

After the war, Mort was the only survivor from among his immediate family. He spent several months in a displaced persons camp, but then was able to leave and start out on a new life. But first, he made his way back to Salonika and went to his family's home, now occupied by a Greek family. They were not pleased to see Mort, fearing that he would reclaim the home that they had stolen after the Jews had been deported by the Nazis. Mort assured them he did not want the home and that he had no intention of living in Salonika, a city saturated with the sufferings of the Jews. They could keep it. He only wanted to reclaim the items buried by his father before the deportation. The Greek family gave permission, relieved that they could keep the house that they had stolen.

Mort dug up the metal box that had been buried so reverently by Yehudah Barbanel. He tucked it under his arm and left without saying goodbye. He arranged to travel to the United States, being sponsored by some cousins who were then living in New York. He got on the boat and never looked back. He would begin a new life in America. He would bring his family's history and traditions to the New World and would continue the family line for generations to come.

Strangely, Mort did not open the metal box right away. He had a powerful yearning to open it; but he also had a mysterious fear. The contents of the box were the remnants of his former life, a life that had been wrenched and tortured by the vicious anti-Semites. However, once Mort had steady employment at his cousin's fruit market, and once he had the privacy of his own living quarters, he finally decided to retrieve the items his father had stored in the metal box.

Mort found several deeds—a deed to the Barbanel house, a deed to his father's store. Mort tore them to pieces. He did not want anything to do with Salonika, not even to reclaim property that was rightfully his. He found a few family photographs that brought him happy memories of days past, and anguished tears for how tragically those days had ended. He tucked them away in a drawer. There were a few other trinkets of minimum value: his mother's wedding ring; his father's one set of silver cuff links; several golden bracelets; and the gold key.

Mort held up the key and kissed it. "I will not betray you," he whispered. "The Barbanel's will rise again. This key will open new doors for us."

Mort spoke little but did much. Within two years, he left his cousin's fruit market and opened his own dry goods store in downtown New York. He married a beautiful bride in 1948, Sarah Nahmias, whose family also had roots in Salonika. Within the next ten years they had three children, all boys, all bearers of the Barbanel name. Mort and Sarah wanted their sons to grow up American, and they gave them American names. The first-born, named after Mort's father Yehudah, was called Thomas. The second-born, named after Sarah's father Isaac, was called Richard. The third-born, named after Mort's paternal grandfather Yaacov, was called Harvey.

Mort had a knack for making money. He was amiable, competent, soft spoken; he respected his customers and they trusted him. By 1953, he owned an impressive and thriving store on Fifth Avenue. Mort worked seven days a week. Success was his god. He wanted to restore the wealth and nobility of the Barbanel name. The family moved to a spacious and fashionable apartment on Central Park West.

As they grew up, the Barbanel boys attended the Ethical Culture School. They played little league baseball on Saturday mornings. For their Bar Mitzvahs, they barely learned enough Hebrew to recite the blessings on being called to the Torah. The Barbanels attended synagogue services on the first day of Rosh Hashana and on the eve of Yom Kippur.

As they grew older, the boys attended the Fieldston High School. Although there were quotas for Jewish students in the top American colleges, Thomas gained entrance to Harvard, Richard to Yale, and Harvey to Princeton. Mort and Sarah could not have been prouder.

Life was going well for the Barbanels. Mort often

took the gold key in his hand and smiled proudly. The noble Abarbanel family was reclaiming its destiny.

Thomas went on to Harvard Law School and finished near the top of his class. He was offered a plum position with a prestigious New York law firm. He married a lovely socialite, Margaret Asquith, at a civil ceremony at City Hall. Richard went on to Harvard Medical School, graduated with high honors. After completing his residency, he joined a thriving medical practice on Park Avenue. He married Charlene Smith in a Protestant ceremony. Harvey graduated near the top of his class and went into investment banking. He landed a fine position with a major investment firm. He married Mary McCarthy in a ceremony at a Catholic church. Prior to the ceremony, he converted to Catholicism. But the conversion was merely to satisfy his in-laws. He did not have religious faith, and certainly had no faith in Catholicism.

So at age sixty, Mort Barbanel looked back at his life and did not know what to think. He had survived Auschwitz. He had come as an immigrant to America and had prospered dramatically. He and his wife had raised three fine boys, each of whom had achieved so much. The Barbanel family was a classic American success story. But if everything was so right, why did Mort feel that everything was so wrong?

In his heart, he knew the reason for his malaise. He had sworn to restore the Barbanel name, that the gold key would open new doors of greatness for the coming generations. While the Barbanels had done so well in so many ways, they had failed completely when it came to their Jewishness. Mort and his wife had been intent on succeeding financially, on raising their sons as good red-blooded Americans. In the process, though, they had given up all but the most rudimentary of Jewish religious observances. Yes, Mort had shown the gold key to his sons many times. He had explained the noble and glorious history of the family. He had shown himself to be proud of his Jewish identity. Somehow he had assumed that his children would internalize all of his emotion and pride. But they did not. They were raised as Americans, and their Jewish heritage was merely a vestige of a remote family history.

In a moment of great clarity, Mort retrieved the gold key from its box. The key felt cold in his hand, and heavier than usual. Without saying a word to his wife, he took the key with him as he left the apartment. He crossed the street to Central Park and stood at the edge of the rowing lake. He took the key into his hand, raised it to his mouth, kissed it slowly. Then he threw the key as far as he could into the lake. He watched while it plunked into the water. Once the ripples subsided and the waters became smooth again, Mort turned around and walked back home.

He still did not know what to think; but he felt purified.

THE MEXICAN

A MAN FROM MEXICO turned up one morning at the Berith Shalom synagogue on Eldridge Street, in New York's Lower East Side. He had steel grey hair and angry eyes.

Rabbi Benyosef, the kindly elderly rabbi of the congregation, greeted him politely after services and welcomed him to the synagogue. The Mexican scowled: "Give me back my life," he demanded.

Rabbi Benyosef realized immediately that here was a troubled man. "I'm not sure I understand what you are saying. I've just met you now. I haven't taken away your life. I don't even know who you are."

The Mexican stormed out of the synagogue in a rage.

Next morning, he reappeared for morning prayers. He fidgeted and growled the entire time. When services concluded, he came to the rabbi menacingly: "Give me back my life."

Rabbi Benyosef sat the stranger down and calmly spoke with him to see if he could get a grasp of the situation.

"What is your name?" the rabbi asked.

The Mexican pulled out several passports, each

from a different country, each with his photograph, and each with a different name. "You choose," he spat out.

"Where do you live?" the rabbi asked.

"I have no address," he replied curtly. And then he abruptly rose and walked out.

Next morning, the stranger appeared again at morning services. The rabbi again approached him after prayers, and again the Mexican growled: "Give me back my life."

After several weeks of fruitless conversations with him, Rabbi Benyosef was finally able to learn that the stranger had come to New York from Mexico, that he had been divorced from his wife there, that the rabbis in Mexico refused to give him his Jewish divorce papers until he honored his financial obligations to his ex-wife.

Rabbi Benyosef called the rabbi in Mexico and asked about the case. The rabbi reported that this man was problematic, that he owed his wife a considerable sum of money, that he was in the United States illegally, and that he should be convinced to return to Mexico and straighten out his affairs.

Next morning, Rabbi Benyosef spoke with the Mexican and told him that his rabbi wanted him to return to Mexico.

The Mexican went wild. His mouth foamed with white spittle. "They are criminals," he shouted. "They have taken away my life. I can't go back to Mexico. If I go back they will arrest me. I have no wife. I have no family. I have no country. I have no life. Give me back my life."

Each day, the Mexican would show up at synagogue for morning prayers. He became part of the Berith Shalom prayer community. But congregants were unnerved by his constant grumbling and growling. When someone wished him good morning, he scowled and sometimes even spat on the floor.

No one had a clue of what to do with him.

As the weeks passed into months, it was clear that the Mexican's situation was deteriorating rapidly. He wore the same clothes every day, and they now appeared dirty and wrinkled. As far as anyone knew, he was homeless. No one knew how he managed to eat or sleep or stay warm or earn money.

Winter was approaching. He had no over coat, only a fraying sports jacket. Rabbi Benyosef brought him a winter coat one morning and discretely offered it to him when no one else was around. He threw it in the rabbi's face. "I don't need your charity," he growled. The rabbi put some money into his hand; he threw it on the floor. "I don't need your charity. Give me back my life. I can make my own way if you give me back my life."

As the winter days became harsher, Rabbi Benyosef offered to give him enough money to travel to Florida where it was warmer. Perhaps this was an act of kindness; and perhaps it was simply a way to get rid of the Mexican. "I don't need your charity. I don't need to go to Florida. I have my pride, I have my dignity. I need my life back."

"Yes, you need your life back . . . but how can I give you back your life?"

"You know as well as I do," he said, staring at the rabbi as though he were a criminal conspiring to keep something valuable away from him.

"But I don't know, I really don't know. Please tell me."

He looked at the rabbi in disgust and stomped away.

Several more weeks passed. And then, one day, suddenly and without warning, the Mexican did not turn up for morning prayers. Where was he? How could he be contacted? Did something happen to him? Did he leave town? Did he get his life back?

When seven days had passed without seeing the Mexican, Rabbi Benyosef contacted the police to report a missing person. He described the Mexican, explained how he had suddenly disappeared. While he was neither a relative or close friend of the Mexican, Rabbi Benyosef considered himself the surrogate next of kin. After some investigation, the police reported that a man fitting the description of the Mexican was found dead in Central Park. The body was at the city morgue waiting to be identified and claimed. Rabbi Benyosef went to the morgue and was shown the body. Yes, said the rabbi, that is our friend, our brother.

Rabbi Benyosef immediately called the rabbi in Mexico to inform him of the Mexican's death.

Should we have him buried in New York, or should we ship the body to Mexico? Please keep him in New York. Please bury him there.

So Rabbi Benyosef and the morning *minyan* group arranged for the burial of the Mexican in the congregation's cemetery. As the body was lowered into the grave, the rabbi realized he did not even know the Mexican's real name. How could he recite the memorial prayer without knowing the name of the deceased? Rabbi Benyosef improvised: "May the Almighty grant rest to the soul of our friend and our brother, a man whose name we do not know."

THE CEMETERY

YOSEF BENEZRA was a pious, elderly Sephardic Jew who had come to New York from Istanbul in the early years of the 20th century. Being the eldest sibling in his family, he was reverentially known among the Benezra clan as Hermano Yosef. The community at large adopted this title for him and everyone knew him as Hermano Yosef.

Hermano Yosef had a light complexion; his hair was white as snow. His head shook ceaselessly, as though he were constantly saying, "no, no, no." He never raised his voice. He was the epitome of gentleness and goodness. One could imagine that the prophet Jeremiah would have looked like Hermano Yosef, calm, holy, with a sad gleam in his eyes.

Everything about Hermano Yosef's life seemed to have a tragic tinge. He grew up in great poverty in the Balat neighborhood of Istanbul. His parents both died when he was still a boy, leaving him and four younger siblings as orphans. An aunt and uncle "adopted" the Benezra children, but were not happy with the added headaches and expenses that came with them. Once Yosef had reached the age of eighteen, he set off for America. Within a few years, he earned enough money to send for his younger siblings, and all were re-united in New York, where they lived in a tenement on the Lower East Side. Yosef worked day and night to maintain his siblings, and he helped them get through school and find successful ways in life.

Once his siblings were on their own, Yosef found a bride and hoped to start on a new path in life. But his bride died within a year of the wedding, and Yosef was left as a young widower. He never married again.

Not having received much of a formal education, he worked at low-paying odd jobs. He lived simply and frugally. As he grew older, he developed a bad limp in his left leg. His breathing became more difficult and asthmatic. And his head began to shake back and forth uncontrollably, "no, no, no."

Yet, with all his problems, he remained a model of calmness and holiness. "All is for the best," he would say. "Praise the Lord for He is good, His mercy endures forever."

Hermano Yosef found solace in the synagogue. He never missed a morning or evening prayer service. Even after the prayers had been concluded, he stayed in the synagogue to repair old prayer books and re-stitch tattered prayer shawls. He made sure that the synagogue was kept neat and clean, that the oil lamps were always lit, that the Torah scrolls in the ark were set upright rather than tilting to one side or the other. Because of his constant loving presence in the synagogue, people came to see Hermano Yosef as the symbol of religiosity. He always served, and never asked for anything in return. He was a genuine servant of God.

But Hermano Yosef's primary concern was with the community's cemetery. He thought that a society could be judged by the way it treated its dead. A properly maintained cemetery indicated that the community cared about its departed members. It demonstrated that love and respect transcend death. A beautiful cemetery was a reflection of a loving community which loved—and continues to love—its dead. The living and the dead constitute one community.

By the mid-20th century, the Sephardic cemetery was almost filled with graves. Each new death brought sadness not only to the deceased's family, but to the committee responsible for the cemetery; each filled grave meant one less available grave.

The leaders of the community recognized the problem. Committees were formed, suggestions were made; but little actual progress was made. A new cemetery would entail a huge expenditure to buy the land and to build a chapel, as well as the ongoing expense of maintaining the cemetery. The existing Sephardic societies all had budgets of their own to meet, and were reluctant to make financial commitments to a new cemetery.

But even if the committees and societies were slow to act, death did not take a respite. People died. They needed to be buried. Families could not be told that a new cemetery would be available some years from now, once funds were raised. There was no negotiating with a dead body.

As community leaders struggled with this dilemma, Hermano Yosef decided that he personally would take responsibility for raising the funds for a new cemetery. He saw this project as his last *mitzvah,* a final meritorious act of pious devotion before he himself would pass on to the next world. Caring for the dead is an especially great act of piety, since it is done with pure idealism, with no expectation of reward. The dead cannot say "thank you."

Once he began on this mission, Hermano Yosef was infused with newfound energy. He was tireless in his solicitation of funds. "A good name is better than precious oil," he would say. "Contribute generously so that you will share in this great *mitzvah.*" He went to businesses and to homes. He solicited donations from the grocers and garment workers; from shoemakers and storekeepers. He solicited from the rich and from the poor. He would not be put off or rejected. "Please give generously. The honor of our community is at stake. We must care for our dead with reverence and love."

Hermano Yosef could often be seen walking throughout the neighborhood in search of donations. His head constantly shook, "no, no, no;" his expression was serious but sweet; he used his cane as an extra leg to give himself more strength. Everyone marveled at his single-minded devotion. Where did he find the energy? Where did he gain this superhuman persistence?

Hermano Yosef himself contributed generously

from his own meager assets. "I cannot ask others to do what I won't do myself," he explained. "I am ready to sacrifice; let everyone do the same." He had a fire within him that could not be repressed.

When he was within range of his fundraising goal, he went again to a wealthy member of the community who had thus far refused to contribute. Again the wealthy man declined to contribute. Hermano Yosef was undaunted: "You are a rich man, I am a poor man. But I will donate all my assets to the last penny, if only you will contribute according to your means." The wealthy man saw no way out; he made a large donation. Hermano Yosef rejoiced as he withdrew his entire bank account and donated it to the cemetery fund. The goal had been reached. The cemetery committee bought land for the new cemetery and had a new chapel constructed there.

The day arrived for the dedication ceremony and a large crowd gathered at the cemetery for this historic occasion. Hermano Yosef was quietly congratulated and thanked by many. In a special way, this was his day. He had completed his last *mitzvah* with singular devotion. No one else could have or would have made this day possible.

The time came for the dedication of the chapel. The chairman announced that the cemetery committee had voted unanimously to name the new chapel in honor of the wealthy man and his wife who had made a fine donation to the cause. The chairman offered profuse praise of this philanthropic couple and their visionary leadership, and then unveiled a handsome plaque with the names of the wealthy man and his wife. Everyone applauded and congratulated the philanthropists. Hermano Yosef was quickly forgotten, standing alone on the new cemetery lawn. The rich man, after his donation, was still a rich man. Hermano Yosef, after his donation, was penniless.

In the days ahead, Hermano Yosef retained his pious demeanor. He showed no frustration, anger or bitterness. Perhaps his head shook "no, no, no" with a bit more sadness than usual.

"Everything is for the best," he said. "Praise the Lord for He is good, His mercy endures forever."

When Hermano Yosef died a year or so later, he was among the first to be buried in the new cemetery. He had no assets with which to pay for the funeral, so he was given a pauper's funeral paid from the funds held by the cemetery committee. At the burial, there was no *minyan* present for the recitation of Kaddish.

"A good name is better than precious oil."

GOOD AND EVIL

RALPH BENVENISTE worked hard to become a doctor. He grew up among working class Turkish-Sephardic immigrants and children of immigrants, most of whom lived in the Central District of Seattle. As a teenager, he attended Garfield High School where he excelled in all his studies, especially science classes.

Ralph was handsome and amiable, a decent athlete, a quiet and responsible student. Everything about him exuded promise and success. His years at Garfield were happy.

Except for one thing.

He had an implacable enemy: Tom Bruckman.

Tom Bruckman was a bully. He could do fifty push-ups—on his fingertips—without stopping. He could do a seemingly endless number of pull ups. His arms and chest bulged with muscle, and he had a short fuse. All the students at Garfield knew better than to tangle with Tom. The least annoyance would cause him to burst into anger; and the anger was usually accompanied by violence. Tom had been suspended from school many times, but he always came back and enjoyed his notoriety. Not only were the students intimidated by him, but the teachers also feared him.

Tom Bruckman was a hater. He hated blacks, Jews, Hispanics, foreigners. He hated smart students. He hated stupid students. He hated anyone who did not look at him with the respect he felt he deserved. He hated anyone who dared stand up to him. Most of all, he hated Ralph Benveniste.

Tom hated Ralph because Ralph was Jewish, because Ralph's family were Spanish-speakers, because Ralph's grandparents and elder relatives were foreign-born, and because Ralph was extremely smart. But mostly he hated Ralph because he thought Ralph didn't respect him.

Tom went out of his way to harass Ralph. He looked for opportunities to bump into him or push him, to taunt him. Although Ralph was a strong young man, he knew he was no match for the muscle-bound thug. Ralph, like many other students, did his best to avoid Tom. But barely a week went by without Tom causing grief to Ralph.

Ralph did not report Tom to the principal or school officials. He did not tell his parents about the problem. He did not discuss the matter with friends. He kept it to himself. He pretended not to hear the taunts or to feel the bumps and shoves. He pretended not to hear Tom's laughter or to see his arrogant and defiant smirk. He thought of Tom as he would think of a rabid dog: this was a menace to avoid, not to confront directly.

One day after gym class, Ralph was in the locker

room getting dressed when Tom came up to him and loudly accused him of stealing his towel. Ralph continued to dress without replying to the charge. Tom shouted and called Ralph a thief, a cheating Jew, a conniving foreigner. A crowd of students gathered around.

Ralph made some quick mental calculations. To take this abuse in the presence of classmates was intolerable. But to fight back was suicide.

In an instant, Ralph picked up his wet towel and slapped Tom across the face, full force. "Here's your towel, scumbag!"

The crowd of students gasped. Ralph was gutsy, but he was a goner.

Tom now had an excuse to attack . . . and he did. He punched Ralph in the face and in the stomach, striking quickly and surgically. Although in pain, and knowing he could not possibly win the fight, Ralph swung at Tom's face, connecting right on the nose and causing Tom to bleed. The crowd of gawkers went wild. They had never seen anyone fight back against Tom, and they surely had never seen Tom bleed.

By Ralph's great good fortune, the gym teacher came into the locker room just then and was able to break up the scuffle before Tom could strike back. But Tom swore revenge. And Ralph did not doubt the seriousness of the threat.

Word spread quickly that Ralph had drawn blood from Tom. Students were awed by Ralph's courage.

But, of course, they could not display their approval in the presence of Tom, since Tom would then peg them as his enemies. Ralph, though, sensed the new level of respect he had gained in the eyes of his classmates.

At the next student council elections, Ralph was elected President of the student body. He was elected class speaker. But the more Ralph succeeded, the more Tom seethed with hatred.

Ralph made it a habit of walking with groups of students, never alone. When he heard loud footsteps behind him, he quickened his pace to get away. He was constantly vigilant. Tom was his worst nightmare.

After school one day, Ralph was walking to the bus together with friends. Suddenly, Tom appeared and challenged him to a fight. Ralph kept walking. His friends peeled away one by one, leaving him walking alone. Tom followed, shouted slurs, pushed Ralph from behind.

"You're scum Tom, and a bully," said Ralph is a soft steady voice. "I'm not going to fight with you."

"And you're a punk and a coward," blurted Tom, as he tightened his fists.

Ralph did not reply but attempted to keep walking toward the bus. Tom pushed him again.

"I told you, I'm not gonna' fight with you. If you want to hit someone who isn't going to fight back, then go ahead. But that would prove that you're a bully. And besides, if you hit me, I'll call the cops."

The crowd of students listened in amazement as Ralph spoke without a trace of fear. They watched to see what Tom would do. In the end, Tom did nothing more than spout off a few curses. He walked away tall and proud as though he had won a prize fight; but his image plunged in the eyes of the students. Ralph's courage and intelligence had defeated Tom.

Ralph Benveniste graduated from Garfield among the top ten students in his class. He was class speaker at graduation, and won awards from the Lions Club, the Rotary Club, and the Elks. He was accepted to the University of Washington with a full scholarship.

Tom Bruckman graduated from Garfield with barely passing grades. He won no awards and gained no honors. After graduation, he went to work as a mechanic in his uncle's gas station on East Cherry Street.

Ralph was glad to move on to the next stage in his life, a stage that would finally be free of Tom Bruckman. Even though he was generally victorious in his dealings with the bully, the constant awareness of danger had worn on his peace of mind.

Years passed and Ralph continued to be an achiever. He graduated the University of Washington *summa cum laude* and was accepted into its highly regarded medical school, which he completed with the highest honors. He spent his residency at Seattle's Providence hospital, and upon completion of that residency, he was appointed to the hospital's staff. Ralph wanted to open his own office as a general practitioner, but he first wanted to spend a few years as a doctor in the Emergency Room at Providence. He felt that dealing with the most extreme and urgent cases would give him a better grounding in medicine.

One night, an ambulance rushed in a man who had been wounded in a gangland gun battle. The victim was barely conscious, teetering between life and death. Dr. Benveniste was summoned to handle this new patient in the emergency room.

On the gurney, bleeding profusely, was a dazed Tom Bruckman.

Ralph was a doctor. He had taken an oath to heal the sick. He was to treat each patient to the best of his ability. He was not to pass judgment on the moral character of his patients; he was obligated to minister to the sick, whether rich or poor, righteous or wicked.

He quickly had the patient rolled into an operating room. He would have to staunch the bleeding, locate and remove any bullets lodged within the patient, determine whether vital organs were in need of repair. He quickly gowned up and prepared for surgery.

When Tom Bruckman vaguely realized that the doctor was Ralph Benveniste, he mustered all his waning strength: "I don't want this doctor. I want another doctor." When told by Ralph that no other doctor was available, Tom said: "Let me die, then. I won't owe my life to a dirty *Jew* doctor." Then Tom faded into unconsciousness.

The emergency room staff had heard Tom's orders, as had Dr. Benveniste. Protocol was to administer to the needs of the patient in the manner that best conduced to the patient's recovery to health. So Dr. Benveniste gave the instructions, and the team went to work to save the life of Tom Bruckman. After a delicate operation spanning several hours, the doctor had done the best he could to save the victim's life.

As Tom was rolled into a recovery room, Ralph sat down in the doctor's area and needed time to recover himself. He knew he had done his best to save a life; yet he also knew that the life he sought to save was the life of a despicable, violent hater. He wondered if the quality of his surgery had been negatively affected by his visceral dislike of the patient? Should he have walked away from the case after Tom specifically had rejected his services?

Dr. Benveniste had become a doctor in order to bring health and healing to his patients. He prayed that Tom would recover and would regain his health—not because he had any affection for that scoundrel, but because he was a doctor who wanted his patients to live.

Tom Bruckman gradually regained his health. After months of rest and rehabilitation, he was finally released from medical care. He returned to his home and his job. He also began to plot his revenge against those who had shot him.

As weeks passed, though, he became increasingly obsessed with thinking about Ralph Benveniste.

Ralph could easily have let him die on the operating table. Ralph could have listened to Tom's order not to operate on him. But Ralph had done the surgery and now Tom owed his life to him.

That was intolerable.

One day Tom turned up at Providence hospital's emergency room. He asked for Dr. Benveniste. When Ralph finished dealing with a patient, he came out and found Tom waiting for him.

"I see you are alive and well," said Ralph with a nervous smile.

Tom's face reddened and hardened. "I told you not to touch me. I didn't want a Jew doctor operating on me. You didn't listen."

"You should be glad I didn't listen. If I had let you alone, you would have died."

"It would be better to be dead than to owe my life to you."

In a flash, Tom pulled out a pistol and fired point blank at Ralph's head. Dr. Benveniste fell to the floor, killed instantly. While horrified staffers ran for cover, alarms went off calling for the police. When the police arrived a few minutes later, they found Dr Ralph Benveniste's dead body. Next to it was Tom Bruckman's body. Tom had shot himself.

But Tom was still breathing. The emergency room team was called into action. The ranking doctor performed a delicate surgery that spanned several hours. The entire emergency team worked to to save Tom's life.

Tom's condition stabilized. He was sent to a recovery room and the prognosis for his survival was good.

LEADER OF
THE JEWISH PEOPLE

MY FATHER-IN-LAW spent nearly forty years as rabbi of a small congregation in a small town. He gave sermons, taught classes, chanted the services, read the Torah, blew the *shofar*, ran the Hebrew School, did the weddings, officiated at the funerals—everything. He was the Jewish chaplain of the police department, the fire department, the local hospital, the nearby nursing home—everything. He carried himself with the sense of self-importance befitting a man of distinction. He may have been a small-town rabbi, but he thought big.

Eventually, old age caught up with him. He retired as rabbi of his congregation. He was replaced as Jewish chaplain of the hospital. His honorary titles and positions, while important to him, did not fill his time and his life. After forty years as a central figure in his community, he had to cope with a new reality: he was dispensable, he was peripheral, the world could get along just fine without him.

He kept busy. He found work as a part-time rabbi here and there; he did funerals and unveilings; he served as rabbi at various hotels during the Jewish holidays. As the years passed, he became a bit frailer, a bit more forgetful. He did not admit any diminution in his powers or in his authority, but he was slipping.

One night, while driving home from his chaplaincy work at a nursing home in a nearby town, he became disoriented. His car veered from the road and crashed into a ditch. The car was ruined, but somehow he survived with only bumps and bruises. This was the beginning of a downward spiral that led him to the hospital, and then to a nursing facility, and then to a room in an assisted care institution.

His wife stayed with him all day, every day. His children, grandchildren and great-grandchildren visited as often as they could. Friends stopped by to say hello. The rabbi who had been a leader and a guide was now in need of the ministrations of others.

In his mind, he resisted the notion that he was an increasingly helpless patient. No, he was a rabbi and a teacher and a leader. He insisted on wearing a jacket and necktie every day; he offered words of comfort and inspiration to fellow residents, told them stories and made them laugh. Day by day, though, he was becoming weaker, more dependent, more forgetful. For him, every day was *"Shabbos."* He was no longer quite sure if it was morning or evening. He confused his dreams for reality and reality for dreams.

One morning, we received an urgent call from his attendant. "Your father is acting very strangely today. He wants me to dress him in his good black suit and bring him down to the lobby. He says someone is sending a limousine to pick him up. I don't know what to do."

My wife asked to speak with her father. "Good morning, Dad. What's happening there?"

"This is a special day. I've been waiting a lifetime for this."

"What is it?"

"I received a telephone call this morning. They've appointed me the Leader of the Jewish People. They're sending a limousine to pick me up."

"Dad, who called you?"

"I just told you! They called to tell me I've been appointed Leader of the Jewish People. They're sending a limo for me."

"Dad, maybe you've had a dream, maybe you're a bit confused."

"Don't be silly. I'm getting dressed and will be leaving here very soon. I'll call you later to give you more details."

The attendant got back on the phone. "What should I do?"

"Dress him in his black suit. Put him in the wheelchair and roll him to the lobby. He will soon enough realize that no one is coming to pick him up in a limo, and that he was only having a dream. There's no sense arguing with him, since that will only agitate him. Let him have his way on this."

So the small town rabbi of a small congregation got himself showered and shaved, dressed in his best suit, and was rolled to the lobby in his wheel chair to wait for a limousine to pick him up. He was appointed Leader of the Jewish People, and he was up to the challenge. He would not let his people down. They needed him. They finally realized how much they needed him. For so many years, he was hidden away in a small town—his talents all but ignored by the big city *"machers,"* movers and shakers. But now came the moment of truth. They needed him. They recognized his talent and his wisdom.

My wife and I drove out to visit him after our day's work. We arrived late afternoon, and expected to find him back in his room. We found him, though, sitting in his wheel chair at the front entrance of the building. He was still awaiting the limo that was supposed to pick him up. My mother-in-law and the attendant were distraught. They told us that he wouldn't budge from this spot all day. He didn't go to lunch, because he didn't want the limo to wait even a moment for him. He was ready and able to take on his new post as Leader of the Jewish People.

"Dad," my wife said as gently as possible. "No limo is going to come. Let's go upstairs to dinner. You need to eat something."

"I'm telling you, they called me! They're sending a limo for me. I've been appointed Leader of the Jewish People."

"That was just a dream, Dad. No one called you. There is no limo coming for you. You are not the Leader of the Jewish People. But you are our leader, and the leader of so many others. Don't worry, Dad.

We love you, and that's all that counts right now."

My father-in-law was bewildered. His eyes—always so full of confidence—moistened. His face—always so serene and sagacious—grew infinitely, ineffably sad.

"They're not coming?" he asked hoarsely.

"No, Dad, they're not coming. It was just a dream."

"I'm not the Leader of the Jewish People?" he whispered, shaking his head helplessly.

"No, Dad. But you are our leader. It was just a dream. Let it go."

I took the handles of the wheel chair, and started to roll him to the elevator to bring him to dinner. He looked back at the door several times, just in case the limo actually arrived. But there was no limo.

We brought him into the dining room, and sat with him during his dinner. He hardly ate and hardly spoke. He was trying to figure things out, to get a grasp of what had happened today. He asked several times if we could go to the lobby again to see if the limo had come for him. We just nodded quietly. No, we would not go to the lobby. There was no limo. It was all just a dream.

After dinner, we brought him to his room. We stayed a while to see that he was settled down. My mother-in-law—exhausted from her day caring for her husband—left for her home. Before leaving, we reassured him that everything would be fine, that he would get over his disappointment, that he was indeed a great leader.

Within a short time, his condition deteriorated. It was not too long before he died—still waiting for the limousine that was supposed to pick him up. The small town rabbi died, along with his dream of being Leader of the Jewish People.

On the day of the funeral, a "limo" came for him: but it was not a limo, it was a hearse. He took his last ride leading a procession of his family and community, on the way to the cemetery. The small town rabbi had died, together with his dream.

LOVE AND MARRIAGE

THEY WERE TWENTY-ONE years old and madly in love with each other. He asked her if she would marry him. She blushed, hesitated, dropped her eyes.

"Maybe," she whispered. "But I'm not really sure."

They sat together quietly. He held her hand.

They were married a few months later.

Life was good to them. They worked hard, rose from poverty, enjoyed a growing circle of family and friends. Idealistic, religious, socially involved—they were an exemplary couple. They were very happy.

Every so often—perhaps just as a private joke between them—he would ask her if she would marry him. She would blush, hesitate, drop her eyes and say: "Maybe, but I'm not really sure." He would take her hand, and they would sit quietly.

After she gave birth to their first child, and then their second child, and then their third child—he asked her with a twinkle in his eye: "now will you marry me?" And each time she answered: "maybe, but I'm not really sure." They would laugh and hold hands.

When the children began school, when they grew into teenagers, when they entered college—at each milestone he asked her to marry him. At each milestone, she blushed, hesitated, dropped her eyes and said: "maybe, but I'm not really sure."

This dialogue was repeated each year on the date of their wedding anniversary, at their 25th wedding anniversary party, at their 50th wedding anniversary celebration. They were as madly in love when they turned eighty years old as they were when they were twenty-one. Even more in love. Each gray hair, each wrinkle on their faces was a symbol of victory over the trials and travails of life—victories that they had forged together. Life had been very good to them; they were grateful for their many blessings.

On his 88th birthday, he felt a terrible pain in his chest. He was rushed to the hospital in an ambulance, and she sat next to him, holding his hand. He was put in the intensive care unit. After the various tests and procedures, one could see on the doctors' faces that the situation was hopeless. He was dying and could not be saved.

He knew that his life was coming to an end. And she knew this also. She sat next to his bed, holding his hand. He had tubes in his nose and an i.v. in his arm. He was weak, very tired, breathing heavily.

He looked up into her beautiful, loving eyes. He rallied all his strength and he asked in a trembling voice: "Now will you marry me?"

She blushed, hesitated, dropped her eyes and said firmly: "Yes, I will marry you. I am really sure now."

An overwhelming joy filled both of them. They

held hands. They had reached the pinnacle of their happiness.

THE WEDDING

A COUPLE ENTERED my office for a wedding interview. I did not know either of them prior to this interview. They had chosen to be married at our synagogue because the bridegroom was of Sephardic background.

As they entered my office, I realized immediately that this was not a "usual" case. The groom, dressed in a spiffy white suit, walked slowly with the assistance of a cane. I soon learned that he was 82 years old. The bride, giggling and blushing, was in her 70s. She was wearing a bright colorful dress that might have been expected of a woman half her age.

This was to be his second marriage. His first wife had died a few months before our meeting. He had been married to her for many years, and they had children and grandchildren.

This was to be the bride's first marriage.

The new bride explained that she had been the groom's secretary for many years. She had always been wildly in love with him but dared not reveal this love to him. She loved him so much, she did not want to complicate his life or jeopardize his marriage. She bided her time in a world of fantasy romance. The years passed. The prime of her life was spent waiting, waiting to show her love and to feel loved by her boss.

Once the boss's wife died, she came forward and told him how much she had loved him. He was now an old man, walking with a cane, a father and grandfather . . . and a widower. Yet, she loved him with the intensity of a young bride in love with a young bridegroom.

He agreed to marry her.

Did he love her? Was he marrying her out of pity? Had he always known of her secret passion? These questions did not come up in our interview. The answer was: he agreed to marry her. She was gleeful, and he no longer needed to fear the loneliness of being an old, semi-helpless widower.

The wedding took place in our small chapel. The bride wore a white wedding dress. The groom walked down the aisle, aided by his cane. A small group of family and friends gathered for the ceremony and for the reception afterward.

I performed that wedding with mixed thoughts and sentiments. I felt sorry that the bride had sacrificed so much of her life; she might have married another man and had a family of her own. I felt sorry for the bridegroom. He was old, feeble, and a bit amazed at how things unfolded after his beloved wife's death. I wondered about the feelings of family members who attended the wedding.

Yes, it was a happy day, a wedding day; but the occasion was filled with so many unuttered and unutterable emotions.

I never saw them again after the wedding.

But I have never forgotten them.

THE GAZE OF ETERNITY

DEAR ABE,

You surely do not remember me, but we once went out on a date when we were in college—nearly fifty years ago! We have not been in touch since then.

You were a Senior, majoring in philosophy. You wanted to go to graduate school, earn your Ph.D., and then go on to teach at a university. I was a Sophomore, studying world literature. We were introduced by mutual friends who thought we had a lot in common.

We went out for a cup of coffee and spent about two hours talking in the coffee shop. Although this was so many years ago, I have relived that date nearly every day of my life since then. I have reconstructed our discussions innumerable times.

At some point near the end of that date, our eyes connected for a moment. It wasn't more than a few seconds. But we seemed to look into each other's soul with perfect understanding. This was a taste of eternity, of something incredibly pure and beautiful. I had never had that experience before and have never had it since. That few seconds of gazing into your eyes has been a highlight of my life.

I have relived that moment thousands of times. I

like to imagine that this moment was as important to you as it was to me. But I fear that it was not! I fear that you've never given it another thought.

After our date, I returned to the dorm as in a dream. I prayed that you would call me and ask me out again. I longed to look again into your eyes. A day went by, and then a week, and then a month—but you never called. I waited and I cried. I was tempted to call you, but held myself back. It would not have been proper; you would have thought less of me. If you didn't call me, it meant you didn't want to see me again. As painful as that was to me, I realized that you really did not care about me, that the momentary eye-to-eye interlocking did not have the same impact on you as it had on me.

Well, life went on for both of us. You followed your dream and became a famous professor of philosophy. You've written important studies. You married and had children and you live a comfortable life in your university community. Although you are now professor emeritus, you continue to lecture and write. I have followed your career from afar and am very happy for your many accomplishments.

I, too, have lived a good life. I eventually earned a Ph.D. in literature, and have written dozens of successful children's books. I married an academic, a good man, an admirable man. We had two children, both of whom are married and doing well in their professions. When my husband died three years ago, I decided to move to a retirement community in Florida, where I have a nice group of friends and where I keep myself busy at one thing or another. My children (and grandchildren) live in California. I see them periodically, but for the most part, my life centers on my friends and neighbors in Florida.

So why am I writing to you?

I was recently diagnosed with an aggressive form of cancer for which no treatment currently exists. My doctors believe that I have only a few more months to live—at most.

As I prepare to leave this life, I have one burning desire that still haunts me: I want to see you again, I want to look into your eyes, and for you to look into mine. I want to relive that sacred moment that we shared nearly fifty years ago.

I know this is an outrageous request. You probably don't even remember me or know who I am. You have your own life and your own responsibilities in Boston; why would you want to fly to Florida to see a dying old woman? You don't owe me anything, and I know that I have no right to impose on you.

Nevertheless, I make bold to write you this letter. I have nothing to lose at this point. Perhaps if I had written to you (or called you) while we were still in college, our lives might have unfolded very differently. But here we are, separated by a chasm of years . . . and I at death's threshold.

I do not really expect you to respond to this letter. That's fine, I understand. But if by some remote chance you will agree to fulfill my last wish, I will cover all your travel expenses.

Thank you for your kind consideration, and thank you for the memory.

Sara

* * *

Dear Sara,

I was astounded to receive your letter, and I am glad you wrote it.

First, let me tell you how sorry I am to learn of your terrible illness.

Second, let me tell you that I myself am in declining health and my doctor forbids me to travel. So although I much would like to come to see you, I am simply not able to do so.

Most importantly: I well remember you; I well remember our date; I well remember that special gaze. I, too, have relived that moment thousands of times over.

Why didn't I call you back to ask for another date? I was a fool. I was shy and awkward. I was a boring philosophy student lost in the clouds. When I looked into your eyes, I realized that I was totally unworthy to be with you. You were lively, beautiful, popular. You were a literary person, filled with poetry and fantasy. I was a stodgy bookworm; I lacked the most elementary social skills. I was afraid of you. No, I was just afraid of being rejected by you. I thought of calling you many times, but I shook with fear every time I picked up the phone.

My hope was that once I got into graduate school, I would gain more confidence. I thought that I might reconnect with you the following year, or the year after. But life has its own way of unfolding. I met a lovely woman in graduate school, and we drifted into love for each other. We married, and we had (and still have) a very satisfactory life.

I have never forgotten your eyes. I have never forgotten that eternal gaze that made me feel as though I were melting into the universe.

So now we are two old and dying people, separated by about fifty years and by about 1,500 miles. Our lives were what they were, and they were good lives. But there was a road not traveled, a road that might have brought both of us to great happiness and fulfillment.

My dear, Sara, please forgive me for my past foolishness and timidity. Please forgive me for being so unworthy of your love and respect. And please forgive me for not coming to see you now, at your moment of great need.

Please know that I have never forgotten you and will never forget you.

Abe

* * *

Dear Professor,

I am Sara's daughter. Your letter arrived shortly before she died. I read it to her, and she was filled with ineffable joy. Her face radiated a most beautiful happiness. She died with her eyes open, with a smile on her face.

Thank you for your letter. Thank you for having

given my mother this final kindness.

Jessica

* * *

Dear Jessica,

I am Abe's son. Your letter arrived shortly before he died. I read it to him, and he filled with ineffable joy. His face radiated a most beautiful happiness. He died with his eyes open, with a smile on his face.

Perhaps now your mother and my father will meet in the world beyond and their eyes will resume their gaze of eternity.

Ike

AFTER THE BURIAL

DONNA AND LEVI BENVENISTE were a dignified, intellectual and serious couple, married for over fifty years. They attended synagogue services each *Shabbat* morning, always meticulously dressed. They rarely demonstrated much emotion in public; they were private and reserved people.

Levi Benveniste died in his eighties after a short illness. Donna and Levi had no children, and no living siblings; the funeral was attended only by a few friends from the synagogue.

The day of the funeral was cold and rainy. On the ride to the cemetery, Mrs. Benveniste sat silently in the back seat of the limousine, without tears, without an expression of emotion, without words. At the cemetery, the small group of mourners walked to the open grave and watched as the casket was lowered into the earth.

Following the synagogue's custom, each person participated in the burial by casting three shovelfuls of dirt into the grave. Donna Benveniste, as the widow, was first to do so. Even as the dirt thumped onto the casket, she showed no emotion other than her usually serious facial expression. After the others had also participated in the burial, the cemetery staff filled in the grave. The group of mourners stood quietly with their umbrellas, as the rain continued to fall and as the cold seemed to penetrate their bones.

When the grave was filled, the rabbi recited the appropriate memorial prayers and asked people to return to their cars for the ride home. The rabbi was standing next to the widow and whispered that it was time to get into the car.

But Donna Benveniste did not move toward the car. She stayed at the foot of her husband's grave, pensively, increasingly distraught. After a bit of time passed, the rabbi quietly asked her if she would like to return to the car. She did not reply. She remained standing silently, as the cold rain intensified.

The rabbi did not want to intrude on her mourning or on her thoughts . . . but it was rainy and cold, and it was time to return home. After a few more minutes, he started to move toward the car and had hoped that she would follow his lead. She did not. She remained standing at the grave.

After a few more minutes, the rabbi spoke gently to her: "Donna, it is time to return to the car. It is very cold. It is raining. It isn't healthy for you to stand here in this weather. It is time to return home."

Donna Benveniste suddenly broke out in tears. Crying uncontrollably, she said: "I can't leave him here alone in the cold and rain. I can't just leave him here like this!"

The rabbi stood holding her arm for another few minutes. Eventually, she regained her composure and started her walk to the car for the ride home.

She realized clearly that her beloved husband, Levi Benveniste, was not coming home with her. She realized clearly that she could no longer protect him from the cold and the rain . . . and that he no longer needed her protection.

UNCLE MOSHE'S HOUSE

BITS AND PIECES OF LIVES, bits and pieces of memories.

My father's eldest brother, Moshe, lived right around the block from our house at 511 28th Avenue in Seattle. Uncle Moshe and his wife, Aunty Bohora, owned a red brick home on the corner of Jefferson and Temple Place. (Temple Place was later renamed Empire Way and is now Martin Luther King Jr. Way.)

Uncle Moshe spoke in a loud voice. Everything about him conveyed strength and determination. He was known for his hot temper, his stubbornness. He was tough.

Rumor had it that Uncle Moshe had to flee from the Island of Rhodes in the early 1900s. As a teenager, he had been a worker in a bakery in Rhodes. Someone had the temerity to make a nasty comment to him. Uncle Moshe lifted a large iron pan and smashed the man's head open. No one could insult him and get away with it!

When his parents learned what their first-born son had done, they quickly arranged for him to leave for America—to Seattle, where several Rhodes Jews had already settled.

Whether or not this rumor was actually true, it left

a special aura on the character of Uncle Moshe. We all knew that it could have been true! We learned reverence for him; no one wanted to raise his ire.

Uncle Moshe used to call me by a series of nicknames: Marconi, Macaroni, Markooch, Markoocho. Even with all his gruffness, he could be soft and gentle. When I remember him, I envision him with a confident grin on his face, a grin that seemed to say, "I dare you." His advice to me was always consistent: don't let anyone push you around; don't be afraid to take chances; stand up for yourself and for your family.

In the mid-1950s, the city planners decided to make a new highway that would go through our neighborhood. They planned to widen Temple Place in order to create a multi-laned road to accommodate the increasing traffic in Seattle. A problem arose, though, when it became clear that the road would cut right through Uncle Moshe's property.

The city officials approached Uncle Moshe and informed him of the plans. They explained that his house would need to be vacated, and they offered to compensate him nicely to enable him and Aunty Bohora to move to a new home.

"What will happen to my house if I sell it to you?" Uncle asked.

"We will demolish it so that the highway can run through the land unimpeded."

"My house is not for sale," announced Uncle Moshe defiantly.

No amount of persuasion or financial incentive could budge him. It was his house; he loved it; no one could tell him what to do. He was not about to sell his home only to have it destroyed. Certain things in life were worth fighting for: one's own home was one of them.

My father attempted to convince Uncle Moshe of the advantages of selling the house. This was a great opportunity for him and Aunty Bohora. They could receive a handsome price for the home and buy a new, better one—and still have money left over as profit. Moreover, there was no point in being stubborn, since the city will build its highway with or without Uncle Moshe's consent. You can't beat City Hall.

"You don't understand," explained Uncle Moshe. "This is America. This isn't a tyranny. In America, people are free; we have rights. We can't let people throw us out of our own home."

The highway planners were able to settle with all other home owners whose property would be affected by the construction of the highway. Uncle Moshe was the only holdout.

In frustration or desperation, one of the engineers came up with an idea to break the impasse. He made the following suggestion: the city would not buy Uncle Moshe's house and would not demolish it. Instead, it would have the entire house lifted and moved some yards back so that it would be out of the way of the new road. The city would cover all the costs, would pay Uncle Moshe for the land it would need to expropriate, and would provide money as compensation for the inconvenience caused to Uncle Moshe and Aunty Bohora.

Uncle Moshe was exuberant. "Who said I couldn't beat City Hall?" he gloated.

And so it was. A construction company went to work, lifted the house onto huge beams and moved it out of the path of the new road. Uncle Moshe had won a great victory.

Although the house was relocated only a few yards back, Uncle Moshe thought that everything had changed. He complained that the house had been damaged in the moving process. He complained that the view from the kitchen window was different. He felt that the house had lost its former charm and character.

As Uncle Moshe looked out his window at the construction of the highway, he began to realize that the world outside his house was changing. More people, more cars, more noise, more air pollution. He had wanted to live in his home as it had been— on the quiet corner of Jefferson and Temple Place. But now there was to be a steady stream of traffic passing right by his house. No more peace, no more quiet, no more life as it used to be.

It was not too long after the completion of the highway when Uncle Moshe died.

The first funeral I ever attended was the funeral of Uncle Moshe. I was twelve years old. Our family entered the funeral chapel on Twelfth Avenue and

Alder. A large gathering of relatives and friends had gathered to pay their final respects to Uncle Moshe.

I saw the casket in front of the room, but did not know what it was. I asked my father what was in the box. "Uncle Moshe is in there," he answered somberly.

I was perplexed. "How did Uncle Moshe let anyone put him in a box?"

"He can't fight anymore," my father said softly.

And that is when I first started to understand what death was.

THE INNER CHAMBER
OF THE KING

"EVERYONE WANTS to enter the inner chamber of the palace in order to be in the presence of the King. But the inner chamber is not easily accessible. How will the people find their way to the King? How will they fulfill the yearning of their soul to be in the King's presence?

The palace has many doors. In front of each door is a key. Each key is the wrong key! It will not fit into the door. Those who come to the palace's outer doors must pick up a key, and then go from door to door until they find the one that will be opened by their key. This may take weeks, or months, or even years. When they succeed in opening the door, they enter a vast hallway. Across the hall is a seemingly endless row of doors. In front of each door is a key. Each key is the wrong key! It will not fit into the door. Those who cross the hall must pick up a key, and then go from door to door until they find the one which will be opened by their key. This may take weeks, or months, or even years. Some will lose heart. Some will lose patience. Some will turn away from the palace, knowing they will never reach the inner chamber, knowing they will never be in the presence of the King.

Those who manage to find the right door enter yet another vast hallway. In front of them is a seemingly endless row of doors, each with a key in front of it. Each key is the wrong key. Again the people go from door to door with their key, seeking to find the door that will open for them. This may take weeks, or months, or even years. Many will lose heart. Many will lose patience. Many will turn away from the palace, knowing they will never reach the inner chamber, knowing they will never be in the presence of the King.

Those who persevere will find the right door, and will enter yet another vast hallway. Across the way is another seemingly endless row of doors. In front of each door is a key. Each key is the wrong key. And so they must again go from door to door seeking entry. And many will give up the enterprise, with broken hearts and deep remorse. But those who persist will find themselves in a seemingly endless confrontation with new rows of doors, with new keys that are the wrong keys. They will enter one chamber after the other, always to find locked doors in front of them, always to pick up the wrong keys. How will they find the strength to go on? How will they ultimately succeed in reaching the King?

There is one answer, my son. There is only one human being who can direct the seekers of the King, who can lead them to the correct keys and the correct doors. There is only one human being who understands the souls of the people to their very core, and who himself has ready access to the throne room of the King. That person is the Rebbe. The Rebbe guides the souls of his people to the presence of the King. The Rebbe allows the people to achieve their dream.

People who do not have a Rebbe lose their way. They give up after one or two failures. They do not have a loving Rebbe who can guide their souls. These people, Heaven help them, are lost. They will remain distant from the throne of the King. They will live their lives in darkness, even if they think they have light.

My son, this is the role of the Rebbe: to guide the people to the King's throne room, to help them be patient and persistent, to fan the flame of pure faith within them. The people turn to the Rebbe, and the Rebbe cannot fail them. Their lives depend on the Rebbe's guidance. Their souls are in his hands. He cannot forsake them, nor abandon them, nor turn away from them in their quest. The Rebbe teaches them the mysteries of Torah, lifts their spirits, leads them on a journey to the inner chamber of the King's palace.

My son, I am being called to the Eternal Throne room. My time on earth is coming to a close. You are my successor. The people will turn to you as their new Rebbe. You are brilliant, learned, and wise. You know the people and they know you. I leave for the Throne room with no regrets and no sadness. I have played my role for these many years. And now, I am ready for the next step in my journey. You must be ready for the next step in your journey. Be strong and have courage. The Lord will guide you."

With these words, the great Rebbe of the Dveiker Hassidim passed to his eternal reward. His son, the new Rebbe, stood dumbfounded and forlorn. He was the new Rebbe; but he had no clue how to choose the right keys, how to enter one chamber after the other, how to reach the Throne of the King. If he did not himself know the way, how could he show the way to others? How was he to face the throng of Hassidim who placed their unequivocal faith in him?

The new Rebbe's father had always trusted his secretary, Reb Shloyme; and so the new Rebbe turned to Reb Shloyme for advice. He confided in the elderly secretary that he was not sure of himself, not sure how he could fulfill the expectations of his throngs of followers.

Reb Shloyme replied: "The Midrash teaches that Moses our Teacher studied Torah with Almighty God for forty days and forty nights. Moses learned every detail of Torah from its simplest meanings to its most esoteric mysteries. After this intensive period of immersion in Torah, God told Moses to descend from the mountain and teach the Torah to the people. With each step down the mountain, though, Moses felt he was forgetting what he had learned. When he arrived near the bottom of the mountain, Moses had forgotten everything! He was overwhelmed by his own ignorance and incompetence. He turned around and ascended the mountain again. He explained to God that he had not remembered the teachings that the Almighty had imparted to him. God responded: 'Go down the mountain and teach the people.' 'But I have forgotten everything,' said Moses. 'Go down the mountain and teach the people,' said the Lord. 'You will remember once you begin teaching.'

This is my advice to you: go and teach the people. As they turn their trusting eyes to you, you will gain power from their faith. You will find inner strength and regain your wisdom. You will know how to lead them to the keys that will lead them to the Inner Chamber of the King."

And so the new Rebbe called an assembly of his Hassidim. He did not know what he would tell them; but he knew that if he did not win their confidence right away, his stature and authority would be diminished. How had his father managed so well for so many years? What was the secret of his charismatic leadership? Even after having studied with his father for so many years, he did not plumb the wellspring of his father's power as Rebbe. The old Rebbe, though, was dead; he could no longer help his son. The new Rebbe reviewed his father's last words again and again. The people turn to the Rebbe and the Rebbe must not fail them. Their lives depend on his guiding them to the King's Throne. If he cannot lead them, they are lost. Woe unto the people! And greater woe unto the Rebbe!

The crowd gathered hopefully. They had loved the previous Rebbe, their source of faith and strength. They wanted to love the new Rebbe, the old Rebbe's own flesh and blood. The crowd broke into a *"niggun,"* singing a wordless song filled with holiness and yearning. The Rebbe walked in front of the assembly. He walked slowly and confidently, as befits a king. He raised his hands to silence the crowd, to stop the *"niggun."*

And then the new Rebbe spoke. He spoke with eloquence and learning far beyond what he had ever been able to do in the past. Thoughts flowed into his mind easily, quickly. He quoted biblical verses and Talmudic passages, the words of Hassidic masters, stories from the Midrash. The Hassidim glowed with happiness. The new Rebbe was a fountain of faith, wisdom, strength. He was a worthy successor to his father. He was as great as—no, he was even greater than—his father. Long live the new Rebbe. He will lead us to the Inner Chamber of the King. He is wise and holy; he has the deepest mind, the grandest heart.

When the Rebbe completed his discourse, the Hassidim went wild with joy. They sang, they danced, they praised their new Rebbe in the highest terms. The Rebbe watched in silence and wonderment. Yes, power came to him when he spoke to the people, just as power came to Moses once he descended the mountain and began to teach Torah. It was an intoxicating feeling to have thousands of people enraptured by one's words. Such great faith and enthusiasm gave strength and enthusiasm to the Rebbe; the people's faith in him was the source of his power.

Reb Shloyme came up to the Rebbe and embraced him. "You see, it was as I said. Once you begin to teach, powers emerge of which you were unaware. *Mazel Tov*. You will lead the people to the Inner Chamber of the King."

The new Rebbe returned home that night filled with bewilderment. He had never imagined what it meant to be a Rebbe, to have so many souls relying on his wisdom and spiritual power. Being the Rebbe had come so naturally to his father. But it surely did not come naturally to him. He knew himself to be unworthy of the faith and trust of his Hassidim. He knew that he did not possess magical powers or supernatural insight. He knew that he absolutely did not know which keys opened which doors, and which doors led to the Inner Chamber of the King. He himself had never entered the Throne Room. He was as blind and lost as all his Hassidim. And yet, their pure eyes turned to him as their guide and master. They ascribed to him powers that he did not have.

He did not wish to continue as Rebbe. It would be a vast deception for him to play a role to which he was not entitled.

In the morning, he went to Reb Shloyme and confessed: "Reb Shloyme, I did not sleep at all last night. I prayed, I cried, I thought as carefully as I could. I know with all my heart that I am not fit to be the Rebbe of the Dveiker Hassidim. I am as ignorant and blind as any of them. Even if I gave a fine discourse yesterday, it was entirely accidental;

I cannot possibly perform so admirably each time I address the community. I don't know the way to the Inner Chamber of the King, and I don't know how I can lead people when I myself am lost."

Reb Shloyme asked: "Do you feel so thoroughly inadequate to be Rebbe? Do you feel it would be a hoax for you to pretend to be their Rebbe?"

The new Rebbe responded: "I am thoroughly unfit to be Rebbe. It would be a hoax for me to pretend to be what I surely am not, and what I surely will never be."

Reb Shloyme laughed happily and heartily. *"Mazel Tov,* Rebbe! These are the exact same words your father uttered when he became Rebbe! *Mazel Tov,* Rebbe! You are surely going to be as great a Rebbe as your father was . . . even greater."

BIOGRAPHY

Rabbi Marc D. Angel is Founder and Director of the Institute for Jewish Ideas and Ideals (jewishideas.org), fostering an intellectually vibrant, compassionate and inclusive Orthodox Judaism. He is Rabbi Emeritus of the historic Congregation Shearith Israel, the Spanish and Portuguese Synagogue of New York City (founded 1654), where he has been serving since 1969.

Born and raised in the Sephardic Jewish community of Seattle, Washington, he went to New York for his higher education at Yeshiva University, where he earned his B.A., M.S., Ph.D. and Rabbinic Ordination. He has an M.A. in English Literature from the City College of New York.

Author and editor of 30 books, he has written and lectured extensively on various aspects of Jewish law, history and culture. Among his recent books are *Foundations of Sephardic Spirituality: The Inner Life of Jews of the Ottoman Empire* (Jewish Lights, 2006), and *Maimonides, Spinoza and Us: Toward an Intellectually Vibrant Judaism* (Jewish Lights, 2009), both of which won Finalist Awards from the National Jewish Book Council. His novel, *The Search Committee* (Urim, 2008) also won wide critical acclaim.

He has recently published a collection of thoughts on the Torah portion of the week, *Angel for Shabbat*

(Institute for Jewish Ideas and Ideals, 2010), and *Maimonides: Essential Teachings on Jewish Faith and Ethics* (SkyLight Illuminations, 2012). He serves as Editor of *Conversations,* the journal of the Institute for Jewish Ideas and Ideals, issued three times per year.

Rabbi Angel is Past President of the Rabbinical Council of America. He is co-founder of the International Rabbinic Fellowship, an association of Modern Orthodox Rabbis. He has served as officer and board member of numerous agencies, including the UJA-Federation of New York, the American Sephardi Federation, the Rabbinic Cabinet of Jewish National Fund, and the HealthCare Chaplaincy. He has won awards from many institutions including Yeshiva University, the Orthodox Union, and the New York Board of Rabbis.

Rabbi Angel is married to Gilda Angel. They have three children and nine grandchildren.